Sophia's Dilemma

Troubled

K T BOWES

Copyright © 2013 by K T Bowes

All rights reserved.

No portion of this book may be reproduced in any form without written permission from the publisher or author.

This is a work of fiction. Names, characters, businesses, places, events and incidents are either the products of the author's imagination or used in a fictitious manner. Any resemblance to actual persons, living or dead, or actual events is purely coincidental.

Join our In Crowd

I'm a believer in 'try before you buy.'
There's nothing worse than forking out your hard
earned cash on a doozy and regretting it.
I don't want stinky reviews. I want you to love my work
and feel like you got value for money.
If you'd like 4 free eBooks, you can join my mailing list
at ktbowes.com
The novels will be delivered to your inbox.

Acknowledgement

This book is dedicated to my scientist daughter, who encourages me with kind words and still emails me the corrections.

Love you Charlotte.

Chapter One

"Yeah? You wanna try it?" The voice caused the smaller boy to back away, dropping his hand to his side.

"Na, bro. Not today."

"Not ever!" The tall man-boy gave his adversary a withering look which left him in no doubt who the alpha male was. "Push me again and you'll be sorry."

"Ok." The other boy, a few minutes ago so cocky and confident but now deflated like a balloon, picked up his bag and blended into the crowd. His face looked downcast and his friends surged around him with excitement. Dane McArdle was a few weeks away from his seventeenth birthday. He was of average height, but his proportions showed he still had a way to go in an upwards direction before he was done growing. His features were handsome and brooding, reminiscent of the father he once loved dearly and whose death scarred his life irrevocably. He hardly ever smiled. Until recently there was little to smile about and the world had been denied the profound transformation of his face, into something less intimidating, a tiny chip in his front tooth representing the only blemish. He pushed his way through the crowd of teenage bodies, going against the flow of people leaving the school building.

The other kids moved out of his way, shrinking back from his reputation more than from the boy himself. His school bag was strung across his body and his hands sunk deep into the pockets of his second-hand grey school trousers. His face, usually an unreadable mask, lit up in a smile that looked unusual on him. His blue eyes danced and sparkled and his lips looked full and pink against his dark hair and skin as he ploughed relentlessly through the crowd and back into school.

"It's Dane!" a younger girl hissed at her friends. "He's so hot!"

"He's trouble!" replied her companion.

"He's the strong silent type. I could go for that," she sniggered.

"He looks happy and that can't be good. Come on. The bus is leaving!" The girls sped off towards the bus stop, Dane's smile adding a whole new dimension to their fantasies.

"Where ya going, bro?" a blonde boy called to him, embarrassed when Dane ignored him and kept pushing on through the bodies. The boy turned and cut a track through the wake that began to close ranks after Dane's passage. He fingered the packet of cigarettes in his pocket but wouldn't dare light up inside school. "*One more dean's detention away from complete expulsion!*" the dean's voice returned to him. He couldn't risk that at the moment, not with nothing else to go to.

He followed Dane to the doors of the art room and watched as the taller boy leaned against the door frame, looking at something – or someone – inside the room. Dane's face lit up like a Christmas tree and there was a serenity about him which made the scraggly blonde boy jealous. Darren heard a gentle girl's voice and Dane's face broke into a wide beam. Darren could only see him from the side, but it was obvious Dane was pleased to see the owner of the voice.

A girl from their tutor class came to the door, fitting herself into a navy school blazer whilst struggling with a heavy rucksack.

"Give it here." Dane easily lifted the strap of the rucksack and swung it over his shoulder. It weighed her down but looked empty on Dane's muscular frame. The girl was pretty, *very pretty*. Darren had liked her since Year 10 when they worked on an English project together. She was polite and considerate, not treating him like the outsider he felt he was. He asked her out on a date and she smiled kindly and told him her parents wouldn't allow her to date until she was sixteen. It was so gently done. There was no, *'get lost, you're an ugly git,'* or *'not if you were the last man on earth,'* none of that. Dane gave him a slap once for talking dirty about her. Suddenly it all made sense if he had the hots for her too.

Sophia Armitage had dark brown eyes with long black lashes and wavy chestnut coloured hair that curled at the ends down near the middle of her back. It swished in her pony tail when she walked or turned her head and in Year 10, it smelled so good. Darren hadn't been able to get close enough since to know if it still did. Her skin was tanned and healthy now, although she looked dreadful a couple of weeks ago after the stabbing. She needed an operation to sort it all out. The word around school was that Dane had been a hero and saved her, but he didn't talk much to Darren anymore. Darren flexed his fingers in temper. *I thought we were mates*, he complained inwardly, knowing he would never do it to Dane's face.

Their friendship group had detonated spectacularly a few weeks ago, leaving the other members drifting around like flotsam. Darren felt vulnerable and angry. *So this is why, is it? Because of this chick?*

"Sandie should have killed you," he chuntered to himself, keeping out of sight. "She liked him for years. You don't get to do this, Sophia Armitage."

"Any news on your mother?" the girl asked Dane and he shook his head.

"No. And I don't want to know. She could have turned him away or got the cops when he got out of prison. But she didn't. Now she's lost her kids. She made her choice."

"But..."

"I don't wanna talk about it."

Sophia's ponytail swung as she finished putting her blazer on and she smiled up at Dane. "Ok, sorry."

Then it happened. Dane bent down and kissed her full on the mouth and she did nothing to stop him. She looked as though she quite liked it. Dane put his hands on her hips and pulled her in close to him, burying his face in her hair and probably breathing in the lovely clean perfumed smell, which Darren craved every time he saw the girl. The blonde boy balled his fists and gritted his teeth, thinking all kinds of awful swear words in his head.

"We agreed," Sophia said quietly into Dane's ear, "that it would be better just to be friends at school."

"School's finished!" he complained and kissed her again before putting an arm protectively around her shoulders and leading her down the corridor, in the opposite direction to Darren.

"Have you heard anything about Sandie?" Sophia turned her face to look up at him and Dane shook his head.

"I've heard she's not allowed back. The cops are charging her with wounding with intent."

Sophia stopped dead. "I'm kinda relieved not to have to see her here. But I feel responsible. If I hadn't head butted her..."

"Then you'd be dead!" Dane's voice was stern. "Wise up, Soph. This started way before you and me. I knew she liked me and I ignored it. She was just my stepdad's niece and as rotten as him. I was never interested. It was always you." Dane reached his hand out and stroked Sophia's cheek with such tenderness it made Darren's eyes bug. His car keys jangled to the floor and he backed away from the corner just as Dane looked his way. Dane reached down and kissed Sophia's upturned lips and then took her arm, moving her along the corridor.

So that's his game then! Darren raged inside his head as he bent down to retrieve his keys. No wonder Sandie was driven to distraction, enough to really hurt the other girl. She fancied Dane since primary school, even before her uncle married his mum. It hadn't stopped her messing around with the other boys in the group, but they had all knew where her real interests lay.

Darren drew the cigarettes out of his pocket and lit one up, satisfied as the poisonous chemicals were sucked down into his lungs. He thought about the other girls in the dwindling group and contemplated seeking them out for some fun. Janine was usually good for a laugh but had begun to get clingy lately, demanding things like movie nights and gifts in return for their fumbled pleasures. Lou was acting weird.

He walked down the corridor, following after Dane and Sophia, puffing at the lighted cigarette. He couldn't resist the urge to jump up and wave the burning white stick underneath the smoke sensors half way down. It took a couple of goes, but eventually the alarms sounded and he whooped and ran off, remembering too late the new security cameras installed just after the stabbing. He ran to his beaten up old car in the student car park, suspecting he had just enjoyed his last day at school. *Ever*.

Chapter Two

"Oh crap!" the Year 12 dean moaned as the piercing noise rang out into the car park. "Don't move!" He just intercepted his best student and wasn't intending to let him escape that easily. "Someone else will sort out the fire alarm. It won't be a real fire. The damn thing's gone off eighteen times in the last few weeks and the insurance company are now refusing to pay for the fire brigade call-out. Look, never mind that, Dane. Where's your application form?"

Dane shifted uncomfortably from foot to foot, his scuffed black school shoes grinding the gravel beneath.

"Why haven't you given it to me yet?" The teacher vented his frustration. "This scholarship would really help you right now. Geez mate, money just to come to school and do Years 12 and 13, why would you not apply?" Dane shrugged and kept quiet, but the man hadn't finished. "Fill in the form I gave you, bring me your birth certificate before Friday and I'll photocopy it. Mr Pearce is a Justice of the Peace, so he can verify it and I tell you what, I'll even post the damn thing myself! *Just do it, Dane!*" The teacher tugged angrily on a shaggy red beard at his throat and peered at the student in front of him, aware the young man was almost a head taller than him. *When did that happen?*

Dane's face remained impassive. It was an expression he perfected during the most difficult years of his life, protecting his tiny siblings from a pseudoephedrine addicted mother and a brutal stepfather, who deliberately got her hooked each time he came out of prison. He said it made her more obliging.

Alex Moeras gritted his teeth and stared the young man down. "I mean it, Dane. I know you've got a lot on at the moment. But I want to help keep you in school."

"Yes, sir." Dane's voice was expressionless in the face of the man's angst.

The teacher relented and stepped closer. "Look, I admit it, your results can't hurt my statistics. The rest of your graphics class are...of dubious quality. You can lift my credibility just by putting your name in the right place on the exam paper, which is more than the rest of them will manage." He smiled at Dane and it appeared as more of a grimace. He looked hopefully down at the elfin-like girlfriend. The pair looked cosy and relaxed in each other's company. She seemed like a nice girl, not that Alex ever taught her. He stared at her appealingly. "Can you make sure he does it? I need to get it in the post by this Friday. Otherwise, it's too late."

Sophia smiled back at the dumpy, red-haired man with the tiny eyeglasses which made him look like a blind mole. She daren't nod in agreement, unsure if she could ever make Dane do anything he didn't want to. With an awkward smile, she broke eye contact and moved around to the passenger side of the car, watching a blonde boy from her year lope across the gravel with a lighted cigarette. Alex wagged his finger at Dane and in a threatening voice, told him, "Friday at the latest, first thing in my office. *Don't make me come and find you!*"

Dane flung his school bag and Sophia's into the back of the car and climbed in, slumping back against the seat and raising his arms above his head. Sophia watched him as his shirt exposed a swathe of muscular stomach, a little unnerved as he groaned frustration. "Bloody hell!" Dane ran his hands through his dark, wavy hair and thumped the steering wheel angrily with strong, man-sized fists. The steering wheel shook and the car vibrated with the force of his irritation.

Sophia's brow knotted in fear as she contemplated getting back out of the car. Dane's unpredictability terrified her and she watched him with wide, frightened eyes. "Sorry, sorry," he gushed, seizing her right hand as her left one grappled for the door handle. "It's fine; you know I'd never hurt a girl. I'm not angry with you; I'm just angry."

"Because your mate set the alarm off?" Sophia asked, her brown eyes blinking in innocence.

Dane looked at her in surprise. "Is that what he did?" He saw the skinny blonde boy as the teacher railed at him. Darren tore across to his car with a lighted cigarette trailing smoke in his hand, moments after the alarm sounded. There was only one possible explanation. Dane sighed. "No, not that." He pulled Sophia in towards him, holding her tightly. He liked her so much - had done ever since their first day at school as thirteen year olds in Year 9. It burnt into him like a physical pain. He held her because she made him feel whole again – and because he didn't want her to do a runner.

Dane ran his fingers up the side of Sophia's soft neck and pressed his lips to hers. He heard her give a soft sigh as her lips parted willingly for him and the electricity arced between them.

"No," Sophia whispered, breaking the kiss. "Someone might see us."

Dane sighed in frustration. "You're safe. Sandie's not around. The others won't do anything to you. They won't risk it." Dane's face hardened. "Unless it's because I'm not good enough for you?"

"Don't be ridiculous!" Sophia spat, her brown eyes misting with naked anger. "How could you think that?"

Dane sat back in his seat and ran his hand through his hair. "My mum's a junkie, my stepdad's a convicted drug dealer and I voluntarily surrendered my little brother and sister to foster carers. I'm hardly a shining example of clean living, am I?"

"None of that's your fault!" Sophia grabbed his hand back and kissed the back of it. Her lips were soft on his skin and Dane bit his lip at the sensuous feel of it. He took a giant swallow and almost choked on it.

The girl laughed and tossed her hair. "Careful." The anger melted in her eyes, quickly replaced by mischief as she stroked his dark hair away from his face. Dane kept his eyes closed, pinching the bridge of his nose with his free hand. "Tell me what's wrong then?" Sophia shifted across and settled herself sideways on his knee, wincing at the jab of the gear lever against her painful thigh.

"Still hurting?" Dane asked, saddened by the slight nod and the way her face became shrouded in misery. "I'm sorry," he whispered. He reached his arms around her slender waist and exhaled slowly as Sophia slumped over his chest, resting her head against his shoulder.

"It's fine. It's heaps better already. I just need to forget...all that." She kissed the underside of his jaw and Dane swallowed again, running his hands down her waist and along her skirt, feeling the silky stockings under his palm. He bit his lip. As his fingers caressed the softness, exploring under the chunky hem of the school skirt, Sophia halted his wanderings, pressing her hand over his to still his fingers. Dane wrestled with his heart rate and blood pressure momentarily, his forehead against Sophia's curls.

"Distract both of us," she sighed, sitting up and accidentally grinding her bottom against his thighs.

"What if I don't want a distraction," he breathed, kissing her cheek and feeling the heat of her heightened colour.

"You need one." She pushed at his chest. "We both do! Now tell me what's wrong."

Dane exhaled loudly and groaned, tipping his head back against the scarred leather headrest. "It's too hard to explain."

"So try." Sophia planted her lips over his, pulling away at the instant dilation of his pupils. His blue eyes sparkled with danger and she snuggled against him instead.

"Fine!" Dane sounded grumpy and she tensed, sensing the old, reactionary Dane McArdle just beneath the surface.

"I have filled it in – the form for the graphics scholarship – but I can't hand it to him. I don't have my birth certificate and I need it to apply. Like the man says, it has to be a verified copy. I don't have time to get another one, not that I know how anyway, so I can't apply."

"Why didn't you tell him that?" Sophia asked, her voice muffled from the front of his shirt, which snuggled her deliciously. "Mmnn, I love it when you cuddle me," she whispered. "Nobody else does, not since Mum left..." She left the sentence unfinished and Dane wrapped his arms around her, pulling her into him tightly.

"Moeras will think I'm an idiot," Dane answered.

"He will if you don't tell him the truth. He's only trying to help."

"I know. Stupid thing is, I know exactly where it is. I just can't get it, not without going back...there."

Sophia pulled her head out of his embrace, staring up at him. Her eyes betrayed her sadness. "Is it at your mum's place?"

Dane shrugged woodenly, his body stiff and unyielding with remembered pain. "It should be, unless my stepdad's burned the lot in the back yard like he did last time he got out of prison." Dane shuddered involuntarily, remembering his hurried flight with tiny siblings in tow before his stepdad trashed everything, including the art project he spent months on.

"What about your case worker, from Child Services. Can't she go and get it?"

Dane snorted, the sound rich with sarcasm and lack of hope. "Not likely. Not without cops standing either side of her, not after last time! I'm almost seventeen, Soph.

They only worry about the little kids. They don't give a crap about me. Haven't you worked that out yet?"

Sophia sighed and pushed her face back into his warm chest. "I know you're not living at the hostel. You're sleeping in your car, aren't you?" She didn't look at his face, not wanting to damage his fragile ego.

"How do you know?" Dane's voice sounded flat.

"Your hair was still wet first thing and you smelled of soap. Is Mr Pearce letting you shower in the changing rooms?"

She felt Dane's body shift underneath her. "Yeah. Please don't say anything. He nips round early and turns the alarms off and then goes home for breakfast while I sort myself out. If the principal finds out, he'll be in big trouble."

"I could talk to Dad. You could…"

"No. Thanks," Dane added. "I don't want your dad to think badly of me. I don't want him to know."

"Fair enough. So where's the birth certificate?" Sophia asked, trying to change the subject.

"If it's still there, it's in a drawer unit by my bed. I left it in the top drawer with my passport. Can't believe I left it. I was ready for days this time as well. I'm an idiot."

"No you're not. It was stressful and you were taking care of Maisie and Will. It's not your fault. Why don't we..."

"No!" Dane interrupted her before she could state the obvious. "I can't get it, Soph. I'm never going back there. He'll kill me if I set foot on the property. He warned me." Dane's fingers strayed to the scar which criss-crossed his eyebrow, feeling the raised skin, still tender to the touch. "I should get you home. I've got work tonight." He kissed Sophia's soft forehead and breathed in her nearness, knowing it was the only thing keeping him sane.

"What if I came with you?" she asked. "He couldn't do anything to you then."

Dane breathed out slowly and carefully. She was so innocent and sweet it made his building frustration evaporate. He let out a sad snort.

"Are you cross with me?" Sophia's voice sounded small.

"How can I be cross with you? I know you're only trying to help, but you have no idea what kind of man my stepdad is, or what he's capable of." Dane kissed her gently on the lips again, excited to feel her kissing him back. He pulled away with a teasing smile. "I've got work, babe. I need to go. Anyway, the birth certificate doesn't matter. I'm not going back. I'll have to live without the scholarship; it's not worth the effort."

Dane started the car engine and tickled Sophia as she climbed off his knee. She squealed and giggled and after a few disjointed hiccoughs, the old car ignition fired obligingly to life. Dane smiled down at his beautiful girlfriend and drank in the sheer enjoyment of being with her. "Soph?" he said, biting his lip. His courage failed him the instant she looked at him with her expressive brown eyes and his declaration of love sank back into his stomach. "Hey, nothing, don't worry."

He thought she had forgotten all about the birth certificate as he held her hand in between changing gear, but he couldn't have been more wrong.

Chapter Three

"I need to pick something up for Dane." Sophia smiled nervously at the woman at the door of the decrepit house, the following afternoon. It looked derelict, as though nobody lived there, the paint peeling from the wooden window frames and the door barely clinging to its hinges. Sophia had just concluded they must have moved away until with an agonising grind; the buckled front door opened just a crack.

A wizened face peered out into the bright sunshine, eyes with pupils as large as their irises, blinked rapidly in the light. "Sod off. I've nothing for ya. Try the tinny house away down there. We ain't doin' weed no more." A frail, brown arm waved uselessly in no particular direction and the rapid eye movement reached fever pitch. "Go on. Bugger off!" Spittle left through loose lips, spattering the doorframe and making Sophia jump back.

"But Dane McArdle wants something from here."

At the second mention of Dane, his mother's face changed, filling with a pitiful hope. Her sunken cheeks hoisted themselves northwards to the jutting cheekbones in a valiant effort. She made a serious attempt to focus on her visitor and looked eager, if that was the name of the face expression leaking from bloodshot eyes. "Dane?" she whispered softly. "My Dane?"

A gash adorned the bridge of the woman's nose, resembling the damaging trail of a head butt. Sophia looked shifty, remembering the sound of her own forehead hitting Sandie's big nose that dreadful day when the other girl knifed her. She shivered and banished the memory. The cops agreed it was self-defence. Only Sophia couldn't accept that. *She intended to hurt Sandie*. She knew that in the split second the other girl stepped in front of her, oozing menace and jealousy. Sophia forced herself to look at the woman's cuts and gashes, realising they resulted from more than a single head butt. The shell of a mother was battered black and blue.

"Dane?" his mother said again and stepped back so Sophia could enter the hallway. The stench of cigarette smoke and urine assailed her nostrils like chemical warfare, making her cough and raise her hand to her mouth. Another smell accompanied it, acrid and drifting.

Slightly stooped, the woman's dark hair hung loosely on her shoulders. It was tousled and tatty, more than bedhead - unwashed or brushed for weeks. Her eyes were too closed for Sophia to tell if they were blue like Dane's or brown like his siblings', merely slits in her puffy, white face. There was a sense of beauty lost in a wasteful, drug fuelled existence. Now her face and body were equally ravaged. A white tee shirt shrouded a skeletal body, grey and stained. Looking down, Sophia was embarrassed to see the woman wore only a pair of knickers on her lower half. Her legs were scratched and marked as though she had scrambled through thorn bushes recently. The girl averted her eyes self-consciously and tried not to stare at the wreck of a human being.

"Where's Dane's room?" She asked, choking back bile from the stench of the house.

The woman pointed to a door at the end of the hall. "Dane?" she said again.

Sophia hurried forwards, feeling like a character out of *Jack and the Beanstalk*, waiting for the giant to get home and roar, '*Fee, fie, foe, fum.*' The stink inside the room was awful, a heady mixture of sweat and something else Sophia didn't recognise. No part of it smelled like Dane's scent; deodorant and aftershave. *No wonder he didn't want to come back.*

The single bed was rumpled and unmade, the sheets stained and unchanged for weeks. Finding the dresser exactly where Dane described, Sophia put her hand into the top drawer. She dug around in the mess of socks and underwear tangled inside one another. Her fingers contacted something hard like cardboard and she pulled out the black passport with the silver fern on the cover. From inside it, Sophia teased the folded white paper peeking tantalisingly out of its pages. *Dane's birth certificate.*

"Is Dane comin' home?" The woman's face peered in the doorway.

"I don't know." Sophia withdrew the precious documents and faced Dane's mother, slipping them into her blazer pocket in one fluid movement.

"He dun't mean it, his dad. Dane makes him angry." The woman sniffed and wiped her hand across her nose, leaving a streak of blood.

"Right." Sophia gritted her teeth and swallowed her acid retort. Dane still bore the physical scars from trying to rescue his tiny brother and sister a few weeks ago, when the man got home from prison and attacked him.

"I want him home." The woman's eyes turned gimlet hard within their puffy walls and Sophia's heart beat a frantic tattoo in her breast. "Where is he? Where's my son? I need him."

As Sophia attempted to pass her in the doorway, the foul woman leaned across and blocked the girl's way, resting a yellowed hand on the opposite side of the door frame. Sophia halted, fighting rising panic as the woman's acidic breath invaded her nostrils. "I need some cash," she menaced, white spit coursing down her chin with each word.

Sophia registered her brown iris colour in the dim light of the hallway as the woman's pupils shrunk perceptibly, the drug high wearing off as she plummeted from heights unknown to any sane person. Sophia swallowed hard, pushing away random gratitude that Dane's vivid blue eye colour was inherited from his deceased father. Putting her hand inside the top pocket of her blazer, Sophia pulled out the five dollar note for her bus fare home. Her fingers brushed the hard cover of the passport and she bit her lip, needing to get out. She held it gingerly towards the woman, trying not to touch her fingers as the money was snatched eagerly. Dane's mother eyed her with disgust. "What's this?"

"It's all I have," Sophia said, hearing her heartbeat shake her voice, aware suddenly of noises from another part of the house. Somebody else was home. The realisation offered no comfort.

"It's not enough, is it?" The woman's brown eyes were hard and unyielding and she took a menacing step towards Sophia. A door bust open behind the women and Dane's mother changed in an instant, wincing and cowering in terror. A man's bearded face poked into the hallway.

"Where are you, woman?" he spat. "Get in here and watch this. It's nearly cooked." He halted when he saw Sophia, his face hardening from irritation to anger.

"Who's this?" he snapped. "What's she doin' in my room?"

Dane's mother gulped and Sophia was horrified to see a puddle appear on the bare floorboards beneath the woman's feet, as fear made her urinate without control. It was hideous and the teenager understood with incredible clarity, why Dane put Will and Maisie into care. It broke his heart but they were better off.

The bearded face poked further around the doorway, bringing with it a mess of dirty dark hair and a body naked from the waist up, covered in a thick black pelt.

Sophia swallowed and stared at the man. He wasn't how Dane described him and she fought to control the involuntary tremor that rocked her knees. She imagined some evil satanic creature, capable of wrecking lives just by his presence, sporting cloven feet, horns and a forked tongue. But this was just a man. A very nasty, dirty and smelly man, but human nonetheless. Sophia prayed to the God of heaven for courage and wisdom. *And escape.* Then the man shouted, his voice washing over her like an acrid fog and he morphed into an object of terror. Sophia almost added to the puddle on the floorboards as the man's voice rattled her ear drums. "Who *are* you?"

A line of spittle flew from his mouth and landed on the woman's hand. She stared at it blankly as though trying to work out what it was, but she neither moved nor spoke. Sophia shook in every nerve and fibre, but fought to act cool and unruffled as she blagged her way through. "I thought I left something here earlier," she said quickly, keeping her voice even. "But I didn't. My mistake."

She pushed past the woman in the doorway, stepping over the urine on the floor, which drained slowly down through wide gaps in the boards. *So far so good*. Sophia proceeded down the hallway with false confidence, stopping as she wrestled with the cracked front door knob.

Her hands sweated and it slipped in her fingers, spinning back on itself before it fully disengaged the metal lug which kept it clinging to the doorframe. Sophia's head swivelled as she felt hot breath on the back of her neck, either side of her ponytail. To her horror, another man stood right behind her. She turned slowly, aware of the tiny space he left her before she contacted his body. He was the very epitome of evil, a real and physical presence representative of everything wrong with the world. His eyes were hooded by drooping lids and his mouth set in a sneer. *The stepfather*. Dane's mother knew he would be drawn to the noise, the reason for her spontaneous urination. Encountering him, Sophia understood.

The man's eyes were piercing and fully switched on. No chemicals blinded him or caused him to be foggy or caught unawares. He was wiry and thin, his whole body giving the appearance of being sharp, like a blade. His grey hair was slicked back into a neat braid and he wasn't dirty or smelly like the other occupants of the house. He seized Sophia's ponytail, causing her to yelp in pain, dragging her backwards so her face tipped towards the nicotine stained ceiling. The man turned her bodily in front of him, pushing her towards the filthy bedroom, slipping his left hand around her waist in a way that felt familiar and terrifyingly dangerous. "Shh, steady, steady," he hissed in her ear and Sophia felt her heart pound under her blouse, fit to burst clean out of her breast. Dane's warnings ran like cold water down her spine and her breath came in heaves.

She couldn't think properly. Sophia tried to jerk her head backwards in the hope of smacking her captor in the face but he was far too wise and world wary for a move like that. He pulled her hair harder and laughed at the challenge, his nails digging deep into the skin of her neck as he changed his grip. "You must be *Dane's* latest bitch," the man said spitefully, shoving her as she tried to resist, digging the soles of her sensible black school shoes harder into the floorboards and finding no resistance. He said Dane's name as though it tasted unpleasant on his tongue, something eaten that left a cloying taste in his mouth. "Always nice to have Dane's friends visit," the man sneered. "How about I take you in the bedroom for a wee chat then? I bet you'd love that."

The hairy man watched from the doorway, leering, his lips pulled back from pale, rancid gums. Dane's mother continued to stand in her little pool of pee, looking at the ground as though wishing she was anywhere else but here. Sophia knew the feeling. Where were those guardian angels the pastor spoke about in church last year? Surely now would be a great time for them to leap into action. The house was eerily silent. The weakness in Sophia's thigh muscle from the stab wound made resistance more and more difficult as she grew tired and it burned and twinged. Fed up suddenly, Dane's stepfather punched the girl hard in the back with his fist,

SOPHIA'S DILEMMA

tired of her games. "Do as you're told and I won't hurt you. If you're lucky!"

The abrupt crash of the front door slamming against the wall of the scruffy hallway, took them all by surprise. The tricky handle, which only minutes before evaded Sophia, was no match for the figure silhouetted by the sunshine outside the prison-like house. Turning her head she saw him, like an apparition as her hair was yanked painfully backwards. "Get off!" Dane's father yelled as the arm moved forcibly round his throat.

Unable to defend himself and keep hold of the girl, the man let go, throwing Sophia forwards so she landed at the pitiful woman's feet, narrowly avoiding the quickly disappearing puddle.

Dane was a great deal taller than when his stepdad used him regularly as a punching bag. The teenager had matured, gaining bulk and muscle in his manual job and taking the middle aged man by surprise. He easily overpowered his stepfather, dragging him down backwards and deliberately dropping him hard onto his back. The boy's face was a mask of aggression and anger as he straddled the older man and punched him in the face.

"Go!" Dane shouted in between blows and Sophia pushed herself to her feet, taking advantage of the shock on the hairy man's face to slide past the two fighting bodies and make her escape. She flew out of the front door gasping, feeling a clutching sensation in her chest as she fought to breathe. At the end of the street, she turned left, running aimlessly, feeling the new skin on her thigh smarting and objecting to the sudden untrained-for-exercise.

Sophia arrived in the suburb on the bus. Her mother's car, abandoned as she walked out of their lives just after New Year, gave the girl a new found independence and freedom. But the woman appeared a few nights ago and took it back. Sophia's father let her take it, keen to get the sickening female out of his house as quickly as possible. His daughter was devastated when she arrived home from youth group with Dane. Sophia's meltdown was spectacular as Dane pulled off the driveway, his car leaving its familiar streak of oil as a reminder he was there.

"It's ok," Edgar promised, soothing his daughter, brushing loose hair back from her damp, tear streaked face. "Let her take it. I'll sort something out at the weekend. Wait till daylight when she sees all that blood on the front seats. To be honest, I'm glad to see the back of that damn car and its awful memories. At least she didn't take you away from me."

Sophia instinctively ran for the bus stop, sobbing loudly in terror at the same time as cursing her mother for her selfishness. "You even took the car," she raged. "Why do you hate me so much? What did I ever do to you?"

"Are you ok, love?" asked an elderly lady pushing a pram filled with newspapers. She stopped and stared at Sophia, her face full of concern. Sophia gulped and swallowed, nodding like a maniac.

"Boyfriend troubles?" the woman asked, lowering her voice and patting Sophia's shoulder. The girl shook her head.

"No."

"Oh. Are you all right to get home, love?" she asked kindly and Sophia nodded, lying by implication.

The woman smiled, gave her another firm pat on the arm and continued down the street, placing her newspapers in letter boxes along her route. She glanced back occasionally at Sophia and smiled once as the girl heaved for breath and jogged towards the bus stop.

A frenzied wail cut the air like a knife, screeching out a warning as the freight train dashed past, shaking the ground underfoot and rattling everything within a half kilometre of the area. Sophia's thigh pulled tightly from the stab wound as she ran, keeping her hand locked over the precious documents in her pocket. The bus pulled away as she reached the stop, the driver ignoring her raised hand and the young, tear-streaked face. Sophia pulled her arm slowly down to its natural position, realising with dismay the driver had done her a favour. Dane's mother clutched Sophia's only money in her thin, scratched fingers.

With trembling fingers, Sophia pulled her mobile phone from her pocket, desperate to get help for Dane. She ran away like he asked, but couldn't leave him alone and in danger. She dialled emergency and then cancelled the call before it connected. Dane hated the cops and anyone involved in a justice system which allowed him to suffer in such vile and prolonged ways. Pressing her father's number, she readied herself to issue the distress call he always hoped she would never have to make. It went straight to voicemail, telling her he was in a meeting. Her heart sank. "Dad, call me back, please. I need help."

She hovered by the empty bus stop, thinking of Dane with a painful stab of guilt and concern. Her last view of him was the top of his head as he pounded his stepfather's face into a pulp. The image was horrific; his lips set in a firm line, his brow knotted and fists flailing. Two fairly significant punches landed successfully and Sophia heard the awful sound of bone on bone. "I have to go back," she sniffed.

The thought of retracing her footsteps filled her with misery. Her nerves were shot. Sophia's hands shook as she peered at the screen through her tears, clearing her father's number and praying for courage to dial the cops and endure Dane's wrath afterwards. The thought of a second betrayal of him made her weep fat tears. Instead, she turned and ran back in the direction of the derelict house, her school shoes making a slapping sound on the pavement as she bravely returned.

She reached the end of Dane's street when she heard wheels screech to a halt next to her. Terrified, she leapt backwards and ended up half sitting in somebody's hedge. The spiteful branches stuck into the backs of her legs, gouging and scratching. "Get away from me. Get away!" she howled.

Dane emerged from the vehicle, leaving the driver's door open in his panic to get to Sophia. He ran around and tried to embrace her, hurt stabbing like a physical pain in his eyes as she pushed him away, too hard for it to have been just a reaction. "Soph, I'm so sorry. I wish you didn't have to see that." His chest heaved as he tried again, reaching his arms out towards her, seeing what a struggle it was for her to breathe properly. "Oh crap, look at your neck." A set of spiteful scratches and gouges were evident on the right side of her neck, turning from a sickly raised area to red and mottled as the blood rushed back into the violated skin cells. "I could kill him!" Dane wanted to reach out and touch it, to cover it up and pretend it didn't exist, erasing it from memory and physicality. "That he touched you at all makes me sick, but leaving marks makes me wanna kill him. I hate him!" Dane struggled with a deep anger. It burned like a furnace in his soul, dripping hatred down into the hard black residue at the centre of his being, where the horrors and humiliations of his own life hardened into a thick impenetrable crust.

"Why did you go there?" he asked, the words entering the airspace between them as intelligible mutterings. "I told you why I couldn't go back."

Sophia breathed out slowly through pursed lips as though experiencing labour pains and remained sitting in someone's front hedge. She didn't know what to say to Dane, or how to deal with the recurring image of him hitting the man on the ground. The violence seemed relentless. "You were killing him," she sobbed. "You pulped his face and it's all my fault."

Dane's eye blackened in the sunshine and a long cut reached from the side of his nose to the middle of his cheek. It dripped blood slowly down his face and touched his chin before pitching elegantly onto the concrete pavement like a graceful red ballerina. His knuckles were bruised and gashed. Someone tooted their horn angrily at the driver's door, still protruding into the gathering traffic and Dane scooted round to shut it. His movements were heavy and he limped.

"Is he dead?" Sophia asked and her voice was a whisper. "I nearly called the cops."

Dane shook his head, his expression appalled. "No! His mate pulled me off and gave me a hiding. Then they both joined in and I think I bust a rib." He rubbed at an area of his stomach, screwing his face into an agonised wince. "Why did you go there, Soph? I can't believe you did that! And if you called the cops..." he gritted his teeth in anger, "you and me, we'd be done. You know how I feel about them!"

"Thanks!" she shouted at him, taking Dane by surprise. "I went there for you. You told me to go and I got here and was worried sick for you. And now you're threatening me? You go away!" She got up from the prickly hedge and pushed at Dane's chest. "Get away from me. You're just like everyone else!"

Dane's mouth dropped open and his brow furrowed. There was blood in his mouth and Sophia saw it as his tongue shot out to lick his lower lip. It made her feel sick and she bent double, retching into the hedge. "Soph," he whispered, patting her gently on the back. "I'm sorry. I didn't mean it. Nothing would make me dump you. I'm sorry, babe. Listen to me."

"How did you find me?" she sniffed, struggling to maintain her equilibrium and spitting into the hedge without dignity.

"You left your laptop in the car. I got to work and found it so I drove back. I saw you get on the bus at the end of your road and wondered where you were going."

"You *followed* me?" Sophia's voice rose in indignation.

"Yeah, I did. And as it turns out, I'm glad." He patted her back a little too hard and she pushed his hand away. Dane ran his hand through his hair, hissing in pain as he felt the egg shaped lump on the back of his skull. "Bastards!"

Sophia pushed herself to a standing position, batting Dane's hands away. "So, you're blaming me for all this?" she asked, cringing at how pathetic she sounded. "It's all my fault?"

Dane stood up, wobbling slightly on his feet. His eyes seemed to come and go in focus and Sophia looked at him strangely. "Yeah." He nodded, the action making him wince in pain. "Yeah, it is your bloody fault. I told you to stay away. Do you ever listen? The cops stopped me on the way down here for a breath test and road check. If something had gone wrong, I might not have got here in time. Do you honestly think my mother looked like that before he got his hands on her? I can't believe you did this. I'm so angry with you!"

"You still found me!" she sulked.

"Yeah and aren't you lucky!" he snapped. "I just didn't wanna believe you'd be that stupid!"

Sophia's mobile phone trilled out shrilly into the evening air and frightened her. She dropped it and it broke spectacularly into three pieces on the pavement. Dane hissed in pain and wavered slightly as he bent down to retrieve it, salvaging the different parts and managing to fix it back together again. The back of his white school shirt was soaked with blood, garish and freaky in the gentle afternoon sunshine.

Sophia stood silently and watched his long, gentle fingers click the battery back into place and press the sim card into its little slot. She tried to unite the image of these sensitive, arty hands with the fists that pounded the man's face into a bloody mess. The grazes on his knuckles wept clear liquid stained with blood.

Her heart began to pound less and her breathing evened out. When the phone rang again, Dane answered it and handed it to Sophia. His words seemed slurred as he said, "Here, take it. It's your dad."

Sophia reached out and took the phone, her fingers brushing Dane's palm. She felt the surge of electricity between them and felt guilty for what she caused. "Dad, I'm on Bankside Road. Please can you get me?" Her voice broke pitifully but she stepped away from Dane's offered embrace. "Please be quick, Dad. *Please.*"

"I'm not far from there," her father's disjointed voice crackled from the handset. "I'll be a few minutes in this traffic."

Dane waited with Sophia until Edgar drew up in front of them, jumping out of his driver's door, instinctively knowing something was wrong. He held his daughter as she sobbed, looking for an explanation from the bleeding boy in front of him. "What the hell's going on?"

Dane shrugged and looked away. "Ask her," he replied and his voice sounded strange. He climbed back into his car, looking awkward and uncoordinated. With a half-hearted wave, he started the engine and was gone.

Chapter Four

"So you're telling me you violated his trust; went somewhere he stated quite clearly he didn't want you to go and now he's got you out of your stupid mess – you actually think he was out of control?" Edgar listed his daughter's offences on his fingers and sat back in his chair, throwing his knife and fork down on the table loudly. The other people in the café stopped and turned to face the girl and her father, their faces alight with curiosity.

Sophia looked around, embarrassed and surprised at the stance Edgar's stance. "You're taking his side?" Her cheeks flushed with anger, the hysterical tears long since dried on the pretty face. "He pounded the man's face in!" she hissed. "I didn't think he could stop!"

Edgar shook his head in disbelief, a peppering of grey hair amongst the black looking suddenly more prolific. "Have you any idea who these people are?" he asked, incredulous. "They cook 'P' Sophia - pseudoephedrine. You've just told me his mother was so scared she...well, how scared is scared, you silly girl!"

"I don't need this!" Sophia replied angrily, getting up out of her seat and sending it skittering across the floor with a sound like nails on a blackboard. Gritting her teeth, she stomped over to the door of the café and out onto the street, marching off in the general direction of home, ignoring Edgar's shouts behind her. It would be a twenty minute walk if her father didn't manage to catch up with her in his car. "I'll go down the alleys then. Stuff you!" she muttered.

"Hi," said a male voice and turning round, Sophia found herself looking at the blonde boy from Dane's old crowd. She worked with him once in a class years ago and stress erased his name from her brain. "You walkin' home?" he asked and she nodded. "Cool I'll walk a bit with ya." He grinned happily while Sophia struggled to recollect his name, realising he was intent on having a conversation. Her wan smile did nothing to dissuade him and eventually they fell companionably into step, with the boy doing all the talking. *Darren*.

"I just went to me mate's place," he said. "Car ran out of gas, so I went in that cafe for a cold drink for walking home. I'll get the car tomorrow."

Sophia smiled politely and fought to be civil. "Do you live far?"

Darren shrugged. "Yeah. My place is along the road from Dane's. Well, where he used to live."

"Why don't you catch the bus? This is totally the wrong way." Sophia stopped and looked around her for the nearest bus stop. "I might have a couple of dollars…" She groped around in her pockets, remembering Dane's mother holding her last five dollar note in the wasted fingers. Her coffee rose into her throat. "I don't feel so good."

"Na, you don't look it. I'll walk with you for a bit, then shoot off."

"Thanks." Sophia had the decency to look grateful.

Darren blathered on throughout the twenty minute walk to Sophia's Flagstaff house and she listened to very little of it, nodding in all the right places but working to banish the awful images of her visit to the derelict house. "I thought I'd be stood down by today. I set the fire alarms off last night...by mistake obviously. I thought they'd have checked the cameras by now and seen me."

Sophia nodded again and didn't comment. She turned to check the road was clear and her ponytail swung to one side. Darren saw the marks on her neck and let out a low whistle. "Dane rough you up?" he asked, sounding concerned. He spun her round by the shoulders to examine the deep scratches. "Didn't think he was into that."

"No, he didn't," Sophia defended him quickly, pushing Darren's hands away. Something about his touch made her cringe. "It was someone else. Dane sorted it out for me." She bit her lip and wished the teenager would just go away and leave her alone. He showed no sign of doing so.

Darren shrugged and sounded disappointed, "Shame, I was hoping you two broke up. Whoever it was, I bet he fixed 'em good though." He gave a wicked chuckle. "Who was it?"

"I don't want to talk about it." Sophia bit her lip and her eyes filled with tears. They crossed a road, walked up the street and then navigated another alleyway. The suburban back streets were a maze. Darren chatted aimlessly, loping along next to her in shorts and flip-flops. Pale blonde hair spread evenly across spindly legs and his toes were unusually fat.

"Oh, what a mess," she sighed into an awkward silence, missing Dane's capable presence and wishing she handled things differently. Edgar was right. She had been unfair to him. She was the one in the wrong.

"What's up?" Darren stopped in the middle of the pavement.

"Nothing, sorry." Wanting to text Dane and apologise, Sophia fumbled her phone out of her pocket and it fell apart on the footpath once again. "Damn!"

Darren retrieved all the parts and looked at it hopelessly. "Na, you won't be able to fix that," he said, pushing the pieces around in the palm of his hand. "I could probably nick you a nicer one. Want me to?"

Sophia shook her head vigorously, "No, please, don't." Her tone was a little rough and Darren looked hurt. Sophia made a concerted effort to be nicer to him, reasoning it was better to walk with somebody, rather than alone through the alleys and underpasses to her house. At the end of the last grassy reserve of Discovery Park, Sophia turned to Darren and gave him a forced, lovely smile. "Thanks for walking me back. I'm fine from here."

Darren looked reluctant to leave. He flicked his blonde hair out of his eyes and stood awkwardly facing her, fumbling as he reached for her wrists. Sophia knew he was going to kiss her and dodged his hasty movement at the last minute. "Which house is yours?" He sounded hopeful of another try and Sophia cringed inwardly, working hard not to show her distaste.

"My dad will be home by now. He's not in the best mood, so it's best I don't invite you in."

Chastising herself for her inhospitable behaviour, she left him on the pavement and walked towards home, anticipating Edgar's wrath. She knew she would be in a heap of trouble and steeled herself to face the music. The big stucco house was around the next corner and she traipsed towards it, viewing it from the side, her footsteps getting heavier as she went. It wasn't until she turned into the driveway that she came face to face with her father, leaning with his arms folded on the bonnet of a car. His backside rested casually against the bumper as though relaxed but Sophia saw the tiny vein ticking in his neck and sensed trouble.

She stopped dead, preparing her speech in her head – *'Sorry dad for running off, I've just had a rough day,'* no, that wouldn't work, it was far too self-pitying and

Edgar didn't do sympathy. He admitted he didn't find bringing up girls easy. He said it was because he'd never been one. She settled finally on, '*Sorry Dad for running off,*' but the words caught in her throat as she realised whose car bonnet her father leaned on.

Dane's old brown car looked square and tatty against the smart house behind it. Sophia bit her bottom lip and had the decency to look ashamed at the sight of her father's worried face. "I'm sorry, Dad."

Edgar shook his head. "Save it!" He observed her sternly and jerked his head backwards towards the stairs. "In!"

Sophia's feet dragged up the steps and the scar on her thigh pulled as she bent down to take her shoes off. She rubbed at it obviously, courting a little gentleness from Edgar. The action was entirely wasted. He kicked his work shoes off and jammed them in the cupboard by the door and then pushed his daughter in the back to make her go upstairs. It wasn't a hard push or even a jab, but he somehow still managed to convey his great irritation by pressing his fingers into the middle of her back a couple of times. Sophia felt like she was ten years old again and instinctively wanted to throw a paddy, considering leaning back into his fingers and becoming difficult and obstructive. But it was just a fleeting thought. She didn't dare.

Edgar was the family disciplinarian, especially with his son, Matthew. Their mother was the softie. It was ironic really. Such a softie she went missing for over two months while she established herself in a new relationship just around the corner, with another lawyer from her office. Sophia threw herself down on the sofa in the family room, opening her mouth to start issuing her apology whilst wanting to know why Dane's car was on their driveway. Until her mouth started working, she wasn't sure which would come out first. Luckily for her, it was the apology. "I really am sorry Dad," she said, managing to sound genuine. "I shouldn't have walked off like that. It was silly."

Edgar nodded and messed around with the kettle and the tea pot. Then shaking his head, he reached up to the drinks cupboard above the fridge and grabbed a bottle of whisky, pouring a generous slug into a tumbler and sipping it hungrily. "Sod it!" He looked at her with defiance.

Sophia's heart sank, blaming herself for forcing her father to turn to alcohol. If she was a better daughter, things might have been different. Maybe her mother wouldn't have left. She hung her head sadly. "It's ok. I know everything's my fault," she sighed, staring at a line of dangling thread on her skirt.

"Don't start that! Let's not even go there. We'll just deal with this one minute at a time. Your mother made her own choices without even thinking about the rest of us so don't take on responsibility for her! Try sorting your own crap out first." Edgar reached into the cupboard under the sink and pulled out the first aid box they kept for emergencies. Sophia hoped he would tend to her neck, feeling a little softer towards him, but he didn't. He laid it on the work surface and left it there, spewing unopened packets of bandages and gauze.

The sound of a door closing further down the house made Sophia start, her brown eyes widening with hope. Perhaps Matthew had arrived home from his London University, or maybe her mother came to her senses and moved back in. It was a foolish hope, chiefly because Dane's car sat unattended on the driveway. Sophia shouldn't have been surprised when he walked through the doorway from the hall. He glanced at her momentarily but without acknowledgement.

"Let's have a look at you," Edgar stated and they fiddled around in the first aid box. Sophia watched as her father gently bathed Dane's cut lip, the gash on his cheek and a wound to the back of his head. Edgar went over to the freezer and pulled out a cold pack, having to wrestle it from the ice it was welded to and Sophia suppressed a gasp of horror as Dane lifted his shirt up and exposed the dreadful red and black bruising around his ribs. "I think I should take you up to the hospital," Edgar began and Dane pulled his shirt down over the cold pack, shaking his head firmly.

"No. No hospital and no cops."

Edgar shrugged. "Fine. We've got some strong pain killers in the bathroom cupboard." The older man left the room and Sophia heard his socks padding down the hall carpet towards the family bathroom.

Dane stayed still, staring through the window towards the Hakarimata Ranges in the far distance and pressing the cold pack to his bruises through the shirt. His face was a grimace of pain. The hiss of silence assailed Sophia's ears painfully. She couldn't stand it. Getting up slowly, she walked across to Dane, hesitating slightly before facing him and pressing herself into his chest. She heard his lips part with a small 'tut' sound as his ribs compressed, but he put one arm firmly around her and caressed her hair with a shaking hand. "I'm sorry for how I behaved," Sophia whispered. She put both arms around his waist, feeling the cold pack through his shirt as she pushed her nose into his armpit, needing to hide from everything. The leering face of Dane's stepdad seemed to occupy her inner vision and his vicious manhandling left emotional welts on her soul, as well as the physical marks. "I was so scared," she breathed into the fabric of his shirt and Dane shifted his arm to pull her closer, grunting from the movement.

"I know," he whispered. "Believe me, I know."

Sophia wanted to talk about the nastiness in Dane's mother's eyes as she demanded cash in return for safe passage out of the house. But she couldn't, not to the woman's son. "I was so stupid," she sniffed. "I should have left it to you to sort out. And I should never have pushed you away when all you tried to do was help. I despair of myself. I'm a crap daughter and a rubbish girlfriend. How can you ever forgive me?" Sophia felt her tears soak into Dane's shirt, her heart feeling leaden and guilty.

"Let's put it behind us, hey?" Dane stroked her hair one-handed, kissing the top of her forehead. "It's ok, Soph. Of course, I forgive you."

His generosity made the girl feel even guiltier and by the time Edgar returned from turning out the contents of the bathroom cupboard onto the floor, Sophia was inconsolable. She looked hot and bothered, her hair wet from her sweaty, unattractive crying and her dark ponytail had worked itself loose from its bobble.

"Enough now. Leave the boy alone," Edgar snapped at her, still cross as he sent the tablets skittering over the work surface by accident. Searching for another glass, his hand closed around the whisky bottle and he poured Dane a huge slug into his tumbler and pressed it into the boy's fingers. "Let him go for a minute." Edgar peeled Sophia off her boyfriend while Dane drained the glass with the tablets and visibly cringed, shaking his head as the fire burned all the way down to his stomach. It made him want to retch and his fingers clenched so hard around the glass, Edgar reached out to take it from him. He laughed. "It burns I know. But it will cauterise anything amiss inside for sure. And dull the pain. Works for me anyway!"

Dane smirked and put his free hand over the cut on his lip, the alcohol searing the wound and making it sting. The potion worked quickly, numbing the areas it touched and the young man bent double and laid his forearms on the work surface as his head sagged further. Sophia watched in fear, the residual guilt over leaving Dane in the hallway rising to the surface again and overwhelming her.

"I was going back for him," she sniffed into her father's sweatshirt. "I knew he wouldn't want the cops and I couldn't get you, so I ran back to get him."

"Well if you weren't there in the first place, you wouldn't have needed to." Edgar let go of his daughter to help Dane over to the sofa, where he slumped into a curled position over the gap between the cushions. It looked dreadfully uncomfortable. Increasingly worried, Sophia knelt down next to him and rubbed her hand over his bent spine, frightened by the pain radiating from his face. "We should call the cops now though," she suggested, looking up at her father in search of justice. "In case they come after him."

To her chagrin, Edgar laughed openly at her, drowning out Dane's groan. "Oh, what a good idea, Soph," he said sarcastically. "Let's call the cops and tell them you entered a home in order to take something which didn't belong to you and were forcibly detained by the occupants. Then your boyfriend also broke in and assaulted the male of the house, who turned on him in self-defence and beat him up. For goodness sake, Soph, haven't you lived long enough with a defence lawyer to know how it works? A couple of hours later doesn't make the story change."

Sophia looked contrite at the mention of her mother and Edgar wandered off to his bedroom at the other end of the house, leaving them on their own. Dane shut his eyes, waiting for the pain to subside and Sophia stayed on her knees next to him, feeling the familiar tingling and ache as the blood drained out of them. She laid her face against his thigh and dripped sorry tears onto him, feeling the beat of his pulse through the soft skin of her cheek.

Waking up with the side of her nose pressed against the rough fabric of Dane's jeans, Sophia was aware of a dreadful throbbing in her knees. She had tipped forwards so her face was mashed against his thigh and her legs were asleep underneath her. It was excruciating. She gasped as she tipped onto her side and the pooled blood began to pump reluctantly. The numbness was quickly replaced by the awful tingling and then came the agonising ache. Sophia's brain was confused about whether they were her legs or not and she sincerely wished they weren't as they regained feeling.

Voices came from outside in the hallway and as Sophia rubbed at her legs, she heard her father raise his voice in anger. Footsteps, followed by the hall door slamming and then the voices came closer, echoing down the hallway. "You can't do this!" Edgar was shouting.

"Oh no, not Mum," Sophia hissed and held her breath. The door into the family room opened with a crash and Sophia was astounded to see three burly policemen and an equally solid policewoman enter the space. Edgar was right behind them and pushed through their dense bodies towards his daughter. Sophia's eyes were wide and questioning and her father shrugged and shook his head as he crouched down next to her. "It's ok, love. It's all gonna be ok."

The cops looked at each other before one of them unhooked the handcuffs from his belt and the others braced themselves. Edgar raised his hand to stop their progress and leaned over Dane, trying to shake him awake. "Dane, mate, these guys need a word with you." He pointed at the cop with the clanking handcuffs. "He's just a kid. Play nice!"

The teenager groaned as he surfaced from the foggy slumber of constant pain, moving onto his back and crying out. Edgar pushed Dane's hair back from his forehead, finding it damp and sweaty. He shook his head at the cops. "This isn't good. I think he needs to go to the emergency room." He told the woman police officer to flick the light switch next to her and the room bloomed into instant brightness. Sophia shielded her eyes and stared at her boyfriend who was prone on the sofa, a sickly grey colour. Edgar couldn't seem to rouse him and when he carefully pulled his shirt up to retrieve the ice pack, the bruising across his chest and stomach was livid and purple. One of the cops swore loudly and spoke into a small radio on the front of his vest, summoning an ambulance.

The feeling came into Sophia's legs enough for her to kneel up next to Dane and stroke his hair back from his forehead. She kissed his hot, stubbly cheek and whispered, "I'm sorry," into his ear, hoping he could hear and understand her. "I will *never* think I know better than you again."

Edgar raised his eyebrows and tried to suppress the unkind thought which ran unbidden through his brain. Sophia was determined and relentless, just like his wife. The day either of them allowed their men to know better, would be the day Hell froze over and hosted the winter Olympics. He sighed and thought fleetingly of his beautiful wife, choosing to ignore a different man's advice now, instead of his. The cop put the handcuffs back onto his belt. Unless the teenager was a particularly gifted actor, he seriously wasn't going anywhere.

The ambulance was swift and the two paramedics efficient and gentle. Dane was transferred from the sofa to a stretcher with very little fuss. "I know it hurts, mate," one of them soothed as Dane let out a yelp of pain. "We'll get you sorted out soon."

The other paramedic fired a series of questions at Edgar who cringed, colour rising into his dark cheeks. He was forced to admit he gave the sixteen-year-old some prescription drugs belonging to someone else and a decent slug of whiskey, looking extremely guilty and apologetic. "I didn't know he was that bad. I was just trying to help."

Sophia took the opportunity to glare at her father and give him a sanctimonious smile, feeling ashamed as she capitalised on Dane's injuries. She held her boyfriend's limp fingers until moved out of the way while a line was inserted into a vein on top of his hand. The bruises on his face and torso were examined and explained away loosely. Edgar pointed out the wound on the back of the boy's head. "He said he was hit with something sharp and heavy. I'm not very good at first aid. I'm a car salesman..."

"Any slurring of speech or unsteadiness on his feet?" The paramedic glanced up and waited for Edgar to answer.

"Yes. Damn! I wanted to take him to the hospital but he wouldn't go. Geez, I'm sorry." Edgar shook his head and ran his hands through his hair.

Edgar was allowed to travel in the ambulance with Dane, volunteering himself as a temporary next-of-kin for the boy, who fell just weeks inside the protective youth offenders' legislation, but Sophia was forced to remain at the house with the woman officer and one of the men. One cop went in the ambulance to the hospital and the other drove the cop car to meet him there.

As the blue and red strobe lights of the emergency vehicles took off down the main road, Sophia dissolved into tears, surprised when the female officer came up behind her and put her arm round her shoulders. "Come on, love. Sit down." She guided the girl to sit on the sofa Dane had just vacated and Sophia felt the warmth from his body still radiating off the cushions. She stroked it with the palm of her hand, feeling traumatised.

"Is there anyone we can get to sit with you?" the officer asked gently and Sophia shook her head. There was no one. *How sad.*

"Why did you come?" Sophia asked suddenly, wondering why the police unexpectedly turned up at her home. The officers looked at one another fleetingly and Sophia caught the look passing between them. It made her panic. "What is it? Did Dane's mum call you? We didn't break and enter. She opened the door to me and then..."

The male officer handed Sophia a hot drink of tea, more sugary than she liked. Her ponytail flopped forward and he saw the garish nail marks on the back of her neck. He indicated something to the woman with a jerk of his head and she moved, leaning back for a moment to view the spectacle for herself. "You're not in trouble," she crooned, soothing and lulling Sophia with the tone of her voice. "We just need to know what happened earlier today."

The other police officer leaned on the countertop over by the fridge, jotting something down in his notebook as Sophia thought about what she should and shouldn't say. Her mother was a defence lawyer and a very successful one. On the day she mysteriously walked out of her husband and children's lives, she also quit her job, going into partnership with the new man in her life. Edgar rang her old office countless times anonymously without success over the two-month period, hearing only, *"I'm sorry, Sir, she's not here."* On one inspired afternoon a few weeks ago, he admitted he was her husband and got her new phone number.

His wife of twenty-two years had returned to her maiden name of Simpson and hadn't expected her estranged husband to be on the other end of the line. Sally Armitage was one of the best defence lawyers in town and would undoubtedly advise her daughter to say nothing right then. Sophia felt the sting of vulnerability and grew silent, afraid she might say something unhelpful for Dane. It unnerved her how the police just turned up at her house. Certainly Edgar hadn't wanted to let them in - that much was evident from his raised voice on the stairs, but Sophia had seen the handcuffs come out of their holster, clearly intended for Dane.

"I think I would like someone actually," she said, causing the policewoman to raise her eyebrows and look at the man. "Please can you get my Uncle Bob?"

The cops were obliging and kind, allowing Sophia to find the family address book and show the male cop the number to dial. He called it into the control room and they radioed him back in his earpiece a few minutes later. They were much less kind and obliging when the cop turned and informed the room in general that Uncle Bob was on his way. "He said he'd be a few minutes."

In fact, the atmosphere turned positively frosty, despite the balmy evening air. Robert Robertson, or Uncle Bob to Sophia and her brother, was a tall and imposing man of around fifty years old. He arrived wearing jean-shorts and sandals and a tee-shirt from Promise Keeper's which announced, 'I love my wife,' much to the amusement of the male cop who opened the door to him. "Nice tee," he smirked and Uncle Bob smiled jovially back.

"Well, she's a good woman," he responded, offering up the familiar smile which wiped the smug expression clean off the cop's face. Usually, Robert Robertson dressed in an expensively dark three piece suit and matching tie, complete with fob watch and chain. He would remove the fob from his waistcoat pocket and look at it with disdain in the courtroom, usually as he ripped and shredded the credibility of some unlucky police officer giving evidence for the prosecution. It was a sign of feigned boredom and accompanied by that particular smile, caused them to stammer and stutter and destroy their own testimony. In the courtroom, Robert Roberts was feared, but in the fading light of a March evening, he looked positively cuddly.

He ran up the front steps two at a time, maximising his perfect right to be there and blew down the hallway like a flaming backdraught, seizing his slender goddaughter in two very strong, tanned arms. Sophia seemed to sink into him, enjoying the cossetting and protection she knew he would offer. Despite his reputation as a bear in the courtroom, privately he did sympathy extremely well. "I'd like to see my client alone, thank you." His smile was impeccably polite.

The cops were unhappy, maintaining Sophia was neither under arrest nor wanted for questioning. They just required her to fill in some blanks about the incident in Fairview earlier that day and make a witness statement. Uncle Bob smiled nicely. *And refused*. Then he led Sophia gently by the arm into the living room near Edgar's bedroom and shut the door behind them.

"Firstly," he said in a low voice, "it's a dreadful shame about your mother. It took me and Ellen by complete surprise and we're both very sorry about what she's done." He smiled benevolently at the girl in front of him, seeing how beautiful she had become in her teens and sadly, how like her treacherous mother she looked nowadays with her dark hair and eyes, framed by the pale English skin tones. "I've known Edgar and Sally since they first came to Hamilton and I gave Sal her first break as a graduate lawyer. She's worked for me for twenty years on and off, in between having you and Matt. I honestly thought we were friends."

"I don't think it was personal," Sophia offered, rubbing her eyes with trembling fingers. "She dumped us all, not just you."

"Oh, sweetheart. I had no idea your father kept ringing the office, or that he reported the confounded woman missing to the police. I wrongly assumed you all knew and were just licking your wounds..." his voice trailed off, not wanting to admit how the whole of the Waikato law scene were agog with gossip about it. "I should have got in touch. I've been a rotten friend." Sal had not attended a trial since, but Bob was aware the day was looming.

"Now," he said, sitting next to Sophia and keeping his tone soft so the eavesdropping policeman outside the door couldn't hear him. "What can I do for you, my dear? How can I be of assistance?"

"I can pay you," Sophia said softly, "I've got money in my bank."

Bob waved the notion away loftily and in some mock horror, before encouraging the girl to tell him everything that happened, beginning at the conversation regarding the scholarship. When Sophia was finished with her retelling, she looked exhausted and Bob slumped back in his seat on the tasteful cream leather sofa. He chewed on his lip and then picked up the girl's hand, removing it from her lap where it twisted the plaid school skirt until it became a damp, crumpled mess of blue and yellow stripes.

"I made some calls on the way here and pulled in some favours. It seems your young man's stepfather was murdered earlier this evening. A description of you two was given to police as well as Mr McArdle's registration number. The officers have been searching for him ever since. They just struck lucky with the vehicle parked on your driveway. That's how they've ended up here."

Sophia clapped her hand over her mouth in shock and took a huge breath inwards. It was far too big to handle and locked her chest up completely, making her panic as she could breathe in, but not out. Uncle Bob put his hand over her mouth and instructed her quietly to breathe through her nose slowly, in and out, in and out. In the absence of a paper bag, it was all he could think of. He was aware of the ticking clock and growing impatience of the two officers outside the room. "Focus, Sophia," he insisted, pulling her back to reality. "Did this young man kill his stepfather?"

"No!" she stressed in a forced whisper. "He did hit him, but only so I could get away. Then he came after me. He said his stepdad and the other man laid into him. They beat him to a pulp. A dead man couldn't have done that, could he?" Sophia took another deep breath, her chest feeling clearer, but the image of Dane comatose on the stretcher caught her up and she barely suppressed a sob. "He's gone to the hospital. Dad couldn't wake him up, Uncle Bob. He's so sick. He didn't deserve any of this. It's just not fair! It's all my fault and Dad hates me."

Bob squeezed the tiny, sweaty hand and pried the wretched material from her grasp again, patting it and lying it flat on her knee. Then he stood up decisively and smiled confidently down at the girl before him, offering her his hand, palm up. "Let's go and give these Rottweiler's their statement and then we'll get your young man out of trouble."

Sophia statement to the cops was very different in the presence of Robert Robertson, than it would have been an hour earlier and everyone in the room knew it. Sophia told the truth, the whole truth and nothing but the truth, but there was no conjecture, no opinion, nothing which might give them a thread to pull and incriminate Dane. The usual waffly, flowery, artsy teenager was absent from the process altogether, replaced by a woman with a robotic recall of pure fact.

"I went to the house alone. The bus ticket is still in my blazer pocket. Dane's stepfather attacked me and Dane appeared and pulled him off. Yes, I saw him hit the man while they were on the floor but he told me to go and I ran. Dane met up with me on the road by the bus stop. He said his stepdad's mate pulled him off and they both beat him up."

"How long before he caught you up?" The female officer's voice was deceptively soft and Bob gave Sophia a small nod and she answered as rehearsed.

"A few minutes. I ran to the end of the street and missed the bus. A lady asked me why I was crying and I called Dad and then within less than a minute after that, Dane showed up in his car."

"Describe the woman you spoke to."

"She spoke to me. I didn't really say anything to her. She was delivering newspapers in a pram."

All but thirty minutes of the subsequent few hours were accounted for. That thirty minute gap was whilst Sophia and Edgar were in the café and travelled home separately after their argument. Nobody knew where Dane was then.

"So he could have returned to the house during that period?" the woman suggested.

"Speculation officer," Bob interjected. "Please don't lead the witness. You know better than that, or at least *you should!*" He raised his eyebrow at her in a practiced manoeuvre and Sophia saw her cringe visibly.

"What was the row with your father about?" The male police officer scented victory.

"Dad told me off for betraying Dane's trust," Sophia ventured. "Dane said he wasn't going back for the birth certificate and now I understand why."

She described everything in as much detail as she could, including the occupants of the house when she arrived, right down to the dreadful chemical smell about the place. "It was acrid." Sophia wrinkled her nose. "I've never smelled anything like it."

The male officer wrote everything down verbatim and asked her to read it through and sign it, which she did, but only after Uncle Bob read it too and cursorily nodded his head at her. The cops seemed interested in the presence of the hairy man at the property, demanding more details than Sophia could give. "Nobody else mentioned him," the woman said, making Sophia feel like a liar.

"Well, he was definitely there," she maintained. "I've never seen anyone that hairy before." She masked an inappropriate snigger, not wasted on the male cop.

"Lots of firsts for you today then, Miss Armitage." His smile was pleasant but Bob eyed him with disdain.

"We done?" Bob asked with authority and both officers glanced across at each other.

Dane's car was removed for forensic examination, which seemed to affect Sophia deeply as she lost her last contact with him. The cops thanked them politely and left, warning they would return the next day. "They probably want to search the house and garden, in case Dane hid whatever they think he killed his stepdad with. It's unusual they didn't just do it there and then, but I guess it's dark and Dane's going nowhere."

Bob drove Sophia to the hospital and she was glad he wasn't charging his exorbitant lawyer fees by the hour. They found Edgar eventually, mainly through continually texting him and getting lost in the maze of corridors and misleading signs. "I sometimes wonder," Bob interjected crossly, "if there are bored security guys watching the monitors of people going round and round in circles like snails on a wall, getting almost to the right area and then starting again at the beginning. Perhaps they run sweepstakes and tabs on different visitors."

It was a sobering thought, especially as the most lost and bewildered of the visitors seemed to be elderly and distressed.

Dane was in a general surgical ward, but segregated in a room by himself. It would have felt luxurious if it wasn't for the police officer outside his door and the one sitting inside by his bed. Edgar perched on an uncomfortable red plastic chair outside the room, grumbling about how the doctors and cops kept finding excuses to throw him out. Sophia was allowed in for just a few moments while Edgar shook hands with Bob and filled him in on Dane's condition. "Three broken ribs," he said quietly, under his breath so as not to upset Sophia, "which have pushed into one of his lungs and caused blood to pool. They're draining it off and hope it will repair itself without major surgery. It's possible that they can do a keyhole procedure if they need to. The concussion's bad though. I shudder to think how he drove to our place and nobody seems to know where he went between leaving us by the bus stop and ending up back at ours, half an hour or so later. He was already there when I got home, slumped over the steering wheel. Neighbours told the cops he arrived fifteen minutes before me. I don't think he killed the guy. My gut instinct tells me he didn't."

"Wouldn't have blamed him though," Bob leaned in and whispered so he wasn't overheard. "Do they think he'll recover?"

"They're not saying." Edgar sighed and laid his head back against the wall. "He keeps rambling. Kid thinks I'm his real dad, who's been dead over seven years. I'm not sure how to help him."

"That's why I'm here." Bob watched his friend struggle with the notion, nodding once in acknowledgement of his concerns and looking through the half pulled blinds at his goddaughter inside the room. She stood by the side of the bed furthest away from the cop, unable to bear standing next to the wrist that was handcuffed to the side rail of the bed. Dane appeared to be out cold and unreachable but as Sophia stroked his face gently, he stirred and looked up at her bleary-eyed. "Soph, Soph…" he breathed. "I should have…I should have said it…" The handcuffs made a metallic clang as he attempted to reach out. It was pitiful and the two men outside the room saw the agony on the young girl's face, finding the love of her life chained to a hospital bed.

"She seems very smitten, our Soph," Bob commented and Edgar nodded. "It's looking uncomfortably familiar, I suppose."

Edgar threw himself forward in the seat and buried his face in his hands, keeping one eye fixed on the small figure next to her boyfriend's bed. The police officer sidled closer towards Sophia and Edgar's body froze in position as he readied himself to defend her. Bob stretched out an arm to calm him, but it was clear they needed to leave. Sophia bent down and laid her cheek against Dane's. He stirred again and put his free arm around her bent shoulders. The knuckles were cut and swollen, mimicking the blue and purple shades of a rainbow as he stroked Sophia's back with such tenderness. She moved her fingers gently along his face and whispered something in his ear before kissing him and standing up again. It was such a deeply intimate moment, the two men outside the room averted their gaze. The policeman had his arm extended towards Sophia, non-verbally telling her to leave. Dane's eyes closed again, dragging him back to the concussed stupor which hounded and confused him. Sophia turned at the doorway and said in a loud, confident voice, "I know you didn't do it, Dane. I'll prove it." She glared at the policeman and with a flick of her head, left the room, her eyes glittering with unshed tears.

Bob drove Sophia and Edgar home in a silent contemplative journey north, before returning to his wife with the usual spring in his step and an air of being able to sort out just about anything in this life. Before getting into his car on the third floor of the multi-storey car park building, while Edgar waged a silent war on the parking meter, Bob gave Sophia a hug and whispered in her ear, "Just you make sure you get to school tomorrow, young lady."

She looked up at him in amazement, having fully intended to bunk off. He waited until her surprise turned to curiosity before adding, "I think you've got a scholarship to organise, before the cops demand that birth certificate. Otherwise, the whole thing was a waste of time, wasn't it?"

Chapter Five

Despite the ridiculously late night, Sophia was up bright and early to go to school on Friday. To her surprise, Edgar handed her the keys to his posh black SUV and told her to, "Be careful."

"How will you get to work?" she asked him, confused. He smiled widely and she followed him down to the garage, curious.

In the corner of the garage under a tarpaulin, was Edgar's bike. It sat there forever; as long as Sophia remembered. He bought the Harley Davidson eighteen years previously before Matt was born. He kept it serviced, insured and legal, but Sally detested it and after her brother was seriously injured in a motorbike accident more than a decade ago, she forbade him to ride it. "*It's the bike or me,*" she said. So Edgar covered it up and left it hidden away in a corner of the garage, apart from the couple of times a year it visited the engineers behind the showroom he worked at.

"You can't ride that, Dad. Its papers must be out of date. You don't need the police pulling you in over it."

Edgar smirked. "I've been riding this old lady at least twice a year for the last decade. I flexed some hours or took a secret day off to ride it down town and the mechanics knew to get it done before you all came home, so I could ride it back. I rode it in between times too, whenever I could do it without being found out."

"Dad!" Sophia looked shocked. "And you kept it a secret?" Her tone was accusing and Edgar shook his head.

"Don't Soph. Nothing compares to what she did. I got fed up of losing everything to her bullying. This was my only vice throughout all those years of marriage."

He was offered decent amounts of money for it many times over the years and during times of hardship, Sal's beady eyes rested on it as a source of ready cash. But there it still sat, as pristine as the day Edgar bought it from an old guy in Huntly, who looked in the mirror one day and decided his mid-life crisis was over and he looked a prat on it.

"Does it start ok?" Sophia asked doubtfully, brushing dust off one of the smart chrome handlebars.

Edgar produced a rucksack, from which he pulled a pair of leather trousers and a jacket. The rucksack crumpled like a skin to the ground, once the rigid contents were disgorged. "Yep, like a dream," he said happily, fitting himself into the protective clothing over his work trousers and shirt. "Took her down for a warrant of fitness just before Christmas. Today is her lucky day. She's coming to work with papa."

"You sly old dog!" Sophia exclaimed, giggling at her rejuvenated father.

"The only reason I haven't used this bike every day in the last ten years is because of your mother. Now I can do what I damn well like, and I mean to enjoy myself." Edgar squeezed himself into his leathers and did up the zips. He whooped with pleasure. "I've lost weight since last time. I won't need to put my legs down quite as often to breathe at traffic lights. See, there are some benefits to being ditched by the wife!" Edgar pulled the dusty helmet down from a shelf above the bike and fitted it onto his head.

Blowing a kiss to his daughter, Edgar Armitage gave her a cheeky grin that shed years from his face, before pulling the bike out from under the tarp. He lifted it onto its stand while he opened the garage door, starting the engine with a key. It made a lovely, throaty sound as it fired up, suspiciously like it was only ridden yesterday.

Sophia watched her forty-five-year-old father hop onto the huge machine and kick the stand backwards. Then he gunned the engine and shot out of the garage onto the street. He picked up speed as he headed for the junction and his daughter giggled as she saw him punch the air in victory, imagining the loud whoop of joy that would have taken place inside the helmet. "Go, Dad," she smiled, feeling a new found respect for him.

At school, Sophia immediately sought out Alex Moeras, the Year 12 Dean. She had the birth certificate, but no idea where the scholarship form was. "I think it's in Dane's car...which the cops have," she told him.

The astounded teacher slumped down in his chair as Sophia poured out the whole sorry story and he ran his hands through his bushy red hair. Then he stood up decisively. "I'm just going to print another form off," he said with a stroppy edge to his voice. In the doorway, he stopped and looked back at the girl. "You'll just have to fill it in."

Sophia didn't make it to tutor group or art. "Scholarship forms are notoriously difficult," she grumbled. "They make the applicant work far too hard for the possibility of a little bit of help. And it doesn't make it any easier that it's for someone else. I don't know half these answers."

"Make it up, girl," the teacher urged her, watching the hands of the clock tick precariously slowly and wishing morning tea would hurry up and get here. "Possibly don't tell anyone I said that though." He looked momentarily guilty, watching Sophia's every scrawled word and unappealingly scratching his right buttock in nervousness.

The teenager did her best, filling in all the answers and making a much better job of selling Dane as a recipient, than he would have dared do himself. Without the presence of modesty, she managed to make him sound as though they should be grateful for the opportunity to help him.

Alex Moeras read the application form, smiling as he ran a stubby finger down the page, obviously thrilled with the result. He laid it ceremoniously in front of

Sophia on the desk and dropped his final bombshell. "Do you know what Dane's signature looks like?" Sophia gaped and then looked embarrassed. The teacher continued to harangue her, "Well, have you seen him sign anything?"

She nodded slowly, although there was no way she was sharing when, not with the Year 12 dean. Her mind wandered back to last weekend. They sat in Dane's car waiting for the McDonald's drive-through to hurry up and he turned to her and asked, "When we get married, what will your signature look like?"

"I don't know! What a weird question." Sophia was surprised and flushed with pleasure at Dane's assumption.

"Just make one up," he persisted, shoving a receipt from his wallet at her and yanking a pen from the glove box.

"No," she laughed. "I have no idea what it would be."

"Please?" He leaned over and kissed her gently on the lips. "I just wanna imagine." He looked so serious she relented but deliberately did a silly one, making it into a flower.

"That's cute," he laughed. "I'll enjoy watching you do that with all our kids around you and you trying to pay for groceries." He smiled down at the ridiculous *Sophia McArdle* scrawled over the paper and laid his hand on her thigh.

"Have you got a signature?" she asked him shyly and he smiled.

"Course." He scrawled his underneath hers and then stared at the paper wistfully, as though contemplating a time when they really might be Mr and Mrs McArdle. In his distraction, he took his foot off the brake and almost rear-ended the car in front. He didn't mention it again, but put the paper carefully into his top pocket.

Sophia shut her eyes and tried to remember his strong, slanted hand. Then she looked up at the teacher and nodded firmly. He smiled. "I can't actually *see* you do it, for obvious reasons. So I'll just go and copy the birth certificate and get it verified. Then I'll be back."

Returning with his pieces of paper, Alex Moeras was elated with the pretty good impression of something Dane might have produced. Smiling he dismissed Sophia with a bogus note for her art teacher and she progressed to her next class, trying not to worry about Dane.

Edgar rang the hospital first thing but because they weren't family, was only told Dane was 'comfortable.'

But Robert Robertson, as Dane's unofficial solicitor, got much further. He was kind enough to text his goddaughter. *'I'm visiting him later. He had keyhole surgery in the night to deal with the punctured lung and came through it well. I'll be sure to pass on your regards.'* Then he rang his friend.

"She's not eating again," Edgar complained, watching one of his colleagues negotiate a plate glass window, inching an expensive Audi onto the carpeted showroom floor. "I don't want her to get like she did when Sal left. We've only just started getting back to normal."

"Do you think history's repeating itself?" Bob's astute voice came down the line. Edgar nodded and then remembered Bob couldn't see him.

"Yes," he said quietly.

"She's definitely got it bad for him," Bob said, "but for what it's worth, I like what I've heard about him so far. I think it'll be ok."

"Like me and Sal?" Edgar said with sarcasm. "I was her 'bad boy' and I went to a lot of effort to turn it all around. But look at us now. I couldn't stand it if that was my Soph in twenty years' time." He rubbed his hands over tired, blue eyes.

"On the contrary," Bob chastised him, "twenty-two years of a good marriage and two wonderful children cannot be considered a waste! I think even back then, you would have settled for less. Don't write your whole life off, Ed. Just live what you've got left."

Edgar knew his friend was right. He would have traded it all for even two years with Sal and he got many more than that. They were good years too. Just because she ran off and did something out of character, didn't mean the whole thing was a farce.

Sophia went through her day, lonely and friendless, sitting by herself in all her classes. Her ex-friends, Maddie and Heather, avoided her. How strange it was, that she could be friends with someone for more than four years, only for it to fizzle into nastiness overnight for no good reason. Sophia had not been honest with them. Her mother went missing and she kept the whole thing a secret, not even telling the two people closest to her. She doubted they were her friends, frightened to admit her perfect family had suffered a massive landslide and collapsed like a deck of cards. She wondered now what they might have said, had she given them the opportunity.

At interval and lunch, Sophia bolted to the toilets to get in there before the smokers. She failed miserably at lunchtime when the teacher kept the class in for being noisy. Lou and Janine came in after Sophia darted unseen into the cubicle, lighting up cigarettes over by the window and chatting. They cut an oddly lonesome couple without the vicious Sandie in their midst, revolving around Dane's old group of alpha males like satellites orbiting the earth. Even the boys had dispersed nowadays without Sandie and Dane. Sophia tried to be as silent as possible in the toilet, fearful of attracting their vengeful brand of attention.

"Have you told him?" Janine asked Lou and Sophia heard the exhale of cigarette smoke, putting her hand over her nose and mouth as she tried to feed the fallen toilet roll back onto the holder.

"Yes!" came Lou's angry reply. "He says it's not his and he doesn't want to know!"

"That's awful. You can't let him get away with that. Of course it's his. You and him were always doing it. You can't bring a kid up on your own. I bet he was happy enough when you were rolling over for him, but now there's consequences he has to step up. We'll make him," came Janine's sympathetic reply. "Has he said why he won't get involved?"

Lou practically spat out her reply and Sophia heard the venom in her voice, "He doesn't have to, does he? I've seen the way he looks at *her!* I hate her. I wish Sandie chopped her bloody leg right off!"

"Aw, babe. You're not on your own. You've got us and we won't let him get away with this," Janine whispered and there came the sound of Lou quietly sobbing.

Sophia thought she would be physically sick. It was *her* they were talking about. Sandie stabbed her in the leg. Lou was pregnant with Dane's baby. She sat on the toilet seat and put her head between her knees, passive smoking for the whole lunch hour. When the bell finally rang and the girls left the room, Sophia crawled out of her hiding space and wagged off school. She drove down to the hospital and somehow managed to park the huge vehicle in the multi-storey, but the cops wouldn't let her in. She sat outside the ward and cried like a baby. She felt like a massive fool and they wouldn't let her ask Dane for the truth.

With no support network apart from Edgar, who clearly had midlife and desertion issues of his own, Sophia found herself sitting in the Anglican Cathedral on Grey Street. The main doors were thrown open in the heat and various church staff pottered around, allowing her space just to sit, unhindered. The girl envied the Catholics who could wander into their church, hop into the confessional and download all their problems onto someone else. She heard somewhere they were the sanest people around, because of the regular, free, soul unburdening they had access to.

Sophia liked the little Baptist church her family attended. It was slightly outside the city and she grew up in it, loved and cosseted by its congregation of ready-made aunts and uncles, brothers and sisters. The night her mother turned up and took back the car, was Sophia's first night at youth group since before Sal left. Dane drove them and Sophia stuck close to him all night.

It all went horribly wrong as they were leaving and the youth leader asked Dane for his mobile phone number. A kind man in his forties, he had run the youth group through most of his adult life alongside his gentle wife and could be forgiven for scenting the possibility of a conversion. All night, Sophia agonised over telling everyone her mother had left them, but in the end just fudged their well-intentioned questions with shrugs and excuses. She ran smack into Dane's back as he stopped to eyeball the youth leader. "Do you have *her* number?" Dane asked, pointing backwards at his girlfriend.

The youth leader nodded, a fatal mistake, handing his own rejection to Dane on a platter. Dane fixed him with a cold, hard stare. "So how come her ma's been missing for over two months and she hasn't heard from any of you?"

The room silenced and the poor man quailed visibly under the teenager's perceptive gaze. If he knew what was coming, he wisely gave no indication. "I think I'll pass then," Dane said and smiled, reaching back for his mortified girlfriend's hand and leading her out into the warm night air. Sophia said nothing all the way home, finding as she reached her 'safe place' that Sal had taken away the car and with it, her new found independence. Sophia's meltdown was swift and spectacular and Dane left, leaving Edgar to cope with his distraught daughter. "*You've got no-one,*" she said under her breath, hearing her lone voice echoing off the stone around her.

Chapter Six

Sophia sat in the pew so long she figured when she finally stood up; there would be a line on the back of her legs from the hard wooden seat. She heard the traffic noises increasing outside and knew the school mum's were on route to get their little darlings, clogging up the roads and school car parks with their oversize vehicles and 'me first' attitudes.

A woman sat down at the other end of the pew and closed her eyes. Sophia stayed seated, so as not to disturb her by getting off the pew and clumping out in her heavy school shoes. *"Oh, God, please help me?"* she prayed in her head, over and over like a mantra. *"Everything's a mess and I don't know how to sort this. What should I do?"*

She dropped forward so her forearms were on her thighs and sighed heavily. The scar from the stab was still raw when she leaned on it. Sophia pressed deliberately for a second, feeling the sharp pain and experiencing a strange satisfaction from the reality check it gave her. Sitting upright sharply and looking around her, Sophia found the woman's eyes resting on her face. She was attractive, blonde and fair skinned, wearing a red hair band to keep her fringe back. Smiling at the girl next to her, she shivered and said, "It feels cold. I think it might be raining outside."

Sophia nodded. She sat in the church so long she couldn't remember what the weather was like outside. "Rain would be good," she sighed. It would make her feel as though the earth at least cried in sympathy for her. Nobody else would. Sophia looked more closely at the lady and noticed that she wore a grey blouse with a white clerical collar at the neck. Her eyes widened in surprise. She was young and not at all the image of a lady-vicar Sophia had in her head. "You work here?" she asked sharply, regretting the question as it came out of her mouth, sounding challenging and rude.

The woman nodded kindly and asked her where she went to school. They had a short, superficial conversation, just smatterings of small talk really, but the woman was an incredibly good listener. The deeper stuff came once she asked Sophia if she could help her. The girl to her great shame, poured out her myriad problems one after the next until she felt empty and devoid of feeling. The church grew silent around her as people finished their work and crept away, leaving their vicar to work her miracle with the troubled teenage girl.

"So I don't really know what to do now," Sophia tearfully concluded, wiping her eyes on her jumper sleeve and leaving a slug trail of tears. "I feel certain I love him, but this changes things. I mean, we never talked about any of his other girlfriends, so it's not like he lied to me, but it seems to make our relationship dirty somehow. The girl who's pregnant said he won't take responsibility and it makes me doubt him. I didn't think he would ever do that, not after what he's been through; especially when I think how he is with Will and Maisie. Those little kids mean everything to him."

Despite the anger Sophia realised she felt for Dane, she hadn't betrayed his dreadful upbringing to the kind-vicar-lady, glossing over it and cutting straight to the events of yesterday, figuring the woman could draw her own conclusions. "I don't have any blindingly clear answers for you, but..." the vicar smiled gently at Sophia, "if you would let me, I would be honoured to pray for you."

So the teenage girl sat with a total stranger and received comfort and solidarity in her misery. They sat side by side on the pew and the vicar scooted along, not wanting to shout her prayer across the expanse of wood between them. She prayed for clarity for Sophia and God's grace and blessing and she prayed for God's favour to be on Dane right there and then. Sophia sniffed and blew her nose loudly into the tissue the vicar handed her.

"I was going to drive up and see Dane's boss tonight and offer to do his shifts for him until this is all over. Now I don't know what to do. I feel a bit of a fool already and I don't want to make it worse."

"Would that stop him losing his job, do you think?" the woman asked softly. Sophia nodded.

"I thought it would help. I know he needs the money badly. Things are...hard for him."

"So what do you think is the *right* thing to do?" came the vicar's voice. "Is this about him or you?"

"I need to do it, don't I?" Sophia came to her own sad conclusion. "I guess I have to let the past stay there. If he does have a baby with Lou, I'll just have to deal with it when all this is over. I don't think I can still be his girlfriend, but I owe it to him to be his friend."

The vicar smiled sideways at Sophia and nodded, acknowledging the strength and courage in the teenager's decision. Sophia surprised herself by giving the lady a hug before getting up to leave. The woman stayed seated, but as Sophia gathered up her car keys and contemplated driving her father's huge car through the rush hour traffic, the vicar said sagely, "One thing I do have for you, Sophia, are the words -'*This too shall pass*' – that's what I feel to say to you. It's not from the bible, but I also think that Ecclesiastes 3 is relevant for now, '*A time to weep and a time to laugh.*' There is a season for everything and this dreadful one for you, will come to an end. Don't lose your hope."

"Thank you," the girl said, genuinely comforted by the woman's wisdom. "You're right. A couple of months ago it seemed like the end of the world. Mum went missing and nobody knew if she was dead or alive. Fear and dread consumed my every waking moment and now, although my feelings towards her are confused and mostly based on anger and betrayal, it doesn't hurt like it did." There was at least a sense of resolution. Sophia

SOPHIA'S DILEMMA

realised the thing she most needed was resolution - *in everything*.

Sophia was grateful to the vicar for not even broaching the subject of forgiving Sally. She expected it, but the woman left it unsaid. Sophia closed the heavy church door feeling much better and drove Edgar's car north to the garden centre at Rototuna. It took great courage to go in and ask for the manager. The shop was just shutting its doors as she was led to the office and made the acquaintance of a rotund, jovial man, who leapt from his chair to shake hands with her. There was a South African twang to his lilting voice and Sophia liked him straight away. He didn't have a single tooth in his head, but when Harold smiled, it was like the sun coming out on a rainy day, filling the world with a beatific glow.

Haltingly, the teenager explained Dane's predicament and Harold tutted and shook his head sadly. "He does all my potting up in the evenings. I've got a lot ready to be done now. And Saturday's our busiest day, so I'll have to get someone else for tomorrow." He shook his head and looked genuinely upset.

Sophia put her carefully conceived plan to him and he was astounded. "So...you'll do his shifts and then I pay...him?" She nodded. "Why?" Harold asked and it was all she could do not to cry. '*Because he'll have a child to support,*' was what she wanted to say, but she didn't.

"Dane could really use the money right now. And I'm his friend." The words felt like razor blades on Sophia's tongue and the kindly man nodded.

"Yes, I have some understanding of the boy's circumstances."

To the girl's surprise, he agreed. "Be here for eight tomorrow and I'll show you what to do."

Sophia left with mixed feelings and a dreadful ache in her heart.

Chapter Seven

The next day, while the sun still rose and the birds twittered loudly in the overhead trees, Sophia sat in her car outside the front doors of the garden centre, an hour earlier than agreed. She daydreamed and tried not to torture herself with thoughts of Dane and Lou, jumping when Harold knocked on the driver's window. There was an embarrassing moment as the window switch wouldn't work because she took the keys out and as she tried to open the door to speak to him, she hit Harold in his large stomach. "I'm so sorry," Sophia gushed, mortified at her terrible start.

"Na, it's big enough. Don't worry." Harold patted his midriff with a good natured sparkle in his eyes. "Put your car round there, away from the customers." He pointed to a small track at the back of the car park marked 'Staff Only.' Sophia nodded and fiddled with the keys. "Yeah," he commented, "they can garden, but they can't drive."

Sophia had cause to be grateful later that day, when she watched a few of the most avid and knowledgeable gardeners struggle to get their laden vehicles out of the angled parking slots. Edgar would have been livid if she had dinged his SUV.

"She's a darn good little worker," Harold commented to one of the other staff as Sophia lugged bags of compost into the potting area. She was willing and affable, carefully potting the tiny seedlings into bigger trays, exactly as Harold showed her, working quietly in a corner away from the general melee. Mid-morning, he called her for a break over the loud speaker and on her way back to the office Sophia saw an older woman looking perplexed. She stared at a row of large and expensive palms, running delicate fingers over her chin and seeming a bit lost.

"Would you like me to get some help?" Sophia asked, fully intending to fetch Harold or one of the other assistants buzzing around. But the customer launched immediately into her problem and the girl nodded knowingly. "That's exactly what my mum wanted to do," she replied, remembering happier times. "She created a kind of native grove with a bench area and the birds loved it. She copied the design in someone else's front garden and just changed it to fit our garden. The front of our house is very English but out the back is pure New Zealand, like a mixture of the two cultures. It's a neat thing to do."

The woman in her fifties exuded a hurried air that hovered delicately on a state of panic, threatening to pitch over at any second. Looking around her, Sophia noticed the other three assistants deliberately avoiding eye contact with her. "Er, look, I'll write the address down of the garden Mum copied. It's on River Road. If you like it, come back and I'll get someone to help you choose the right plants." Sophia handed the scrap of paper over, adorned with brown fingerprints, an approximate address hastily scribbled on it in pencil. "You'll know it as soon as you drive past," Sophia said and the woman tore off in a hail of gravel to go and see.

The girl wandered to the office and found Harold brewing tea. Elaine, a lady in her late sixties entered the room and slumped into one of the elderly seats. "What did you say to Mrs Barrett?" she asked Sophia casually as

Harold handed out the thick, brown liquid, mouthing 'builder's tea' and giving her a beautiful, toothless smile.

"I sent her to look at a garden design on River Road," Sophia replied. "It'll help her clarify what she wants and then she's coming back."

Elaine rolled her eyes. "Well, *you* can deal with her then. She comes every month with some big project or other and then criticises everything I suggest. She's the worst customer we have and that's saying something. I've been here thirty years and I've seen all sorts!"

"She's the *best* customer we have," Harold corrected. "Her money's as good as anyone's."

Sophia nodded and sipped her tea, agreeing to deal with Mrs Barrett if she came back. She began to doubt she would as they started watering up the millions of pots and planters around the store an hour before closing and she still hadn't returned. Misting the trays of vegetables with a steady stream of water, she was alarmed by a gentle tap on her shoulder and turned, almost soaking the woman who stood smiling at her. Mrs Barrett was back. "I've had a marvellous day!" she gushed at Sophia. "I went to that address and the lady there was so kind. I went in for tea and ended up staying most of the day. Margery's lent me the design for the garden and written down everything I need. She's a widow and my husband's away on business such a lot, so we're going to get together tomorrow and go down to Hamilton Gardens for some more ideas. She's also given me the phone number for her gardener, so I can get him to do the heavy work."

"Wow!" Sophia said, her face lighting up with genuine delight.

"So," Mrs Barrett launched, pushing a piece of notepaper into Sophia's hand, "this is the list of things I'm going to need. Margery said to get the mature specimens even though they're more expensive, because that way I get an instant effect."

"Do you want it all now?" Sophia asked doubtfully, remembering the tiny vehicle Mrs Barrett drove away in. She had listed a six foot Nikau Palm on the paper.

"No, no, Margery's gardener will fetch it all for me in his trailer on Monday. I'll pay up front so you can mark the larger items as sold. I don't want to have to go anywhere else, not now I've decided."

Sophia smiled and led the ecstatic woman over to the queue by the till. Then she fetched Harold and handed him the list. Harold was practically apoplectic with glee at the enormous payment Mrs Barrett happily made, as well as the prospect of shifting some of the huge tree specimens he had long since regretted stocking. But it galled him considerably in his generous heart that the day's wages would go into Dane's bank account and not to the willing little girl who worked all day without a single complaint.

A car sped into the car park five minutes before closing and Elaine at the till rolled her eyes at Sophia, who was loading bags of compost and bark chippings onto a trolley to put inside for the night. A woman and girl dashed from the expensive vehicle and Sophia paid them little attention, busy with wrestling the heavy bags onto the trolley, wondering how many she could get on and still be able to push it.

"Can I take six of those?" the woman's voice asked and Sophia nodded, turning to smile at her. The smile froze on her face and all efforts to rejuvenate it were an epic fail. "Oh, hi Sophia," the woman intoned pleasantly. "I didn't realise you were working here. Maddie and I were gardening and just realised the time. We've nearly finished but need more bark chippings. Maddie can help you load them into the car and I'll just nip in and pay."

With that, the woman was gone, dashing through the sliding doors in a tearing hurry. The girls were silent and uncommunicative as they loaded the heavy bags into the back of Maddie's mother's car, not even getting eye contact in their labour. The woman bustled out of the shop looking considerably happier. "That lovely man was telling me what a good worker you are," she smiled at Sophia. "He also gave me a sizeable discount because I said you and Maddie were best friends."

Sophia put her head down and Maddie looked away, possibly both feeling guilty at the innocence of the lie. The mother looked from one to the other, seeing herself inadvertently blundering into something unpleasant. The pretty dark haired girl in front of her had been absent from her home for some considerable weeks. "How are Sally and Edgar?" she asked, floundering to find safer ground and relieve the tension.

Sophia looked her in the eye and something snapped inside her. "Mum went missing just after New Year. We thought she was dead, but the cops wouldn't look for her. Dad found her recently and she's been on a cruise with her new boyfriend and lives just round the corner from us. She jacked her job in and set up with him. Apparently she's not ready to face me yet." Sophia kept her expression neutral and put her shaking hands on the trolley to stop their jittering.

Maddie and her mother stood gaping like stunned mullets. Telling the truth was releasing for Sophia. It felt good. "Bye then," she said and walked back to the remaining bags, leaving the women stood in the same spot. Eventually they climbed into their vehicle and left.

Hearing the engine race as the car turned into traffic on the main road, a dreadful feeling of anti-climax overcame Sophia and tears dripped off the end of her nose and onto the bags. She wiped them away with the back of dirty, soil encrusted hands, making herself look as though she had war paint on. Harold found her still working twenty minutes after her finish time and shooed her away. He also tried to hand her some cash, but she refused, shaking her tired head and telling him she would be back on Tuesday night to pot up the rest of the seedlings.

Harold watched her leave, saddened by the plight of the young people. She was an excellent worker, but so was Dane. They were both knowledgeable and willing, but Dane had the edge, being exceptionally attractive for the ladies. Harold sighed and then thought about the much healthier bank balance today brought about and smiled to himself, raising his hands to heaven and thanking his generous God.

Sophia drove herself home, running a hot bath and sinking into it until only her face poked out. The hot water was soothing on her aching muscles and absorbed her tears as though they were just a part of the whole.

Edgar and Bob had managed to spend a few minutes with Dane and made the lawyer's representation of him official. He groggily asked for Sophia, astounded when her father told him where she was and what she was doing.

"Dane seemed a little better today," Edgar smiled.

"Oh yeah." His daughter seemed listless and out of sorts. Edgar withheld from Sophia how Dane cried at her kindness, hugely embarrassed by his show of weakness. It was hard for him to remember that Dane wasn't yet seventeen, but had already lived the life of a much older man.

Bob always seemed to know what to say to people. He rubbed Dane lightly on his muscular young back and told him to pack it in, saying kindly, "You'll start me off otherwise."

Dane was recovering quickly from the surgery and his head seemed less foggy, although the banging headache remained. He stayed in the hospital under guard. The cops gave nothing away, baulking as Bob insisted they left the room so he could speak to his 'client.' Edgar tactfully went outside into the corridor and heard the cops complaining. Robert Robertson asked the boy a few questions but mainly encouraged him, giving hope that was mainly fake and partly optimism. "Your mother," Bob told him, "is drying out in a women's shelter. I don't suppose you know the name of the other man at the property? Only you and Sophia mentioned him as far as the cops are concerned. They have no idea who he is." Bob was privately worried they didn't much care either, perhaps assuming the kids cooked him up from nowhere.

"I met him a few times. Real hairy dude but no, I don't remember his name." Dane rubbed at his head and Bob pulled his hand away from the tape holding the wound closed.

"Hey, don't worry. It might come back. Don't force it."

"Would you tell Soph something for me?" Dane asked, concentration on his face.

"Yeah sure." Bob waited patiently.

Dane gulped and hesitated. "Na, it's ok. I need to tell her myself."

"Ok." Bob smiled and shook Dane's bruised hand. "If you're sure."

Dane looked awkward as the police officers returned and he gave Bob a small smile of dismissal. "Thanks, for everything," he said. "In case I don't get another chance to say it."

The lawyer and the car salesman drove north together. The former was buoyant as usual, but the latter was disconsolate and depressed. Edgar noticed the failing light in the boy's eyes and it struck a chord deep within himself. It caused him to relive old nightmares, a desperate and misguided youth coming back to bite him hard.

"You thinking of Sal's dad?" Bob asked with his customary astuteness and Edgar nodded. "Well, stop it. He loved you like a son."

"Yeah, some son." Edgar shifted uncomfortably in the passenger seat. "He saved me from prison, Bob. That gang turned on me, beat me up and left me to take the blame. He got me off burglary charges and gave me hope. I want to do that for Dane but I don't know how. Alan Simpson was a powerful man and I'm not. Did you know he paid for my schooling and everything? I owed it to him to turn my life around."

"And you repaid him a thousand times over!" Bob argued. "He adored you and the kids. He told me, many times."

Edgar thought about his parents, who arrived in New Zealand and then hated it. They turned tail on their emigration, returning home with their dreams in a suitcase. They were still there, happy in the life that sucked them back in like a sinkhole. Alan parented Edgar in their absence, recognising in him a little of his own immigration struggle perhaps. "Thank God the old man isn't around to see me now,' Edgar said out loud as Bob dropped him off on the driveway.

"Stop fretting, Ed. I can see your brain steaming!" Bob shouted and drove away with a roar of his expensive exhaust.

"Well, drive that bloody car nicer!" Edgar yelled. "I sold you that!"

Sophia listened politely to her father's account of seeing Dane but was strangely silent. "How was your day?" he asked and she shrugged.

"Not much point describing it. It's not like I'll be doing it much longer. It's only temporary, isn't it?"

Edgar watched her carefully, aware she was slipping into herself again like when Sal disappeared. It seemed as though she came alive in the company of the young man, but his arrest had affected her almost disproportionately. "Bob will sort it out," Edgar told her reassuringly, pulling her into a hug as she sat on the kitchen stool, sipping a drink he made for her. She had lost too much weight since New Year and he felt her bones sticking through the pyjama top. It bothered him and he wondered if he should mention it. Girls and food were a tricky subject, even he knew that. Not for the first time he wished he could ask Sal how to manage his concerns, but he only saw her twice in almost three months and neither occasion was pleasant.

Sophia ate the toast and jam Edgar rustled up, but her mouth chewed mechanically, her mind elsewhere. After a while, she made her excuses and went to bed early, citing her very physical day for the greyness of her face and the exhaustion which seemed to come from her soul.

Chapter Eight

A knock on the front door around three o'clock Sunday afternoon disturbed Edgar and Sophia as they sat cuddled up on the sofa in the living room, watching an old rerun of a Stallone movie Edgar loved. They enjoyed the morning, visiting the showroom where Edgar worked and sorting out a cheap car for Sophia from the part-exchanges in stock. Picking out a small red saloon being spruced up to go to auction, the showroom owner did her a good deal on it. Sophia emptied her bank account and Edgar fronted up a small amount, just to make it possible.

The owner winked at Sophia as Edgar did the paperwork. "Gotta take care of my best salesman," he joked. "Fifteen years next month. Don't let him leave, hey? I'd be lost without him."

Sophia smiled with pleasure at the compliments showered on her father. Edgar looked embarrassed.

"Put that sale down as your own," he told Edgar. "And throw in a three year warranty on it. Nice little runner that." He waved as he turned to leave and Sophia managed to shout her thanks at him. He winked over his shoulder and limped away, his age beginning to drag him down finally in his eighth decade.

"Nice sales technique, Dad," Sophia laughed. "Is that how you manage to be the best salesman in the company - by buying them yourself?"

Edgar pretended to clip his daughter round the ear and they went for lunch before driving home to watch the movie. Thinking it might be Bob, Edgar threw open the door to find two teenage girls standing awkwardly on the porch. He recognised them, but couldn't quite remember their names, "Er, hi."

The girls tittered childishly, batting long eyelashes at the handsome middle aged man, practicing their budding femininity. Edgar felt awkward. "I'm guessing you're here to see Soph?" he said, inviting them in and leading them upstairs.

Politely offering drinks and finding them declined, Edgar beat a hasty retreat and watched the rest of the movie on an old television in his bedroom. Instinct told him something was definitely going on, but it needed a woman to work out what. "I'm better at being the garbage man," he muttered, "picking up the debris afterwards and clearing the area of all possible trace." He waited a moment for shouts or screams and hearing none, settled down.

Maddie and Heather stayed stood in front of the sofa where Sophia sat, looking shifty and a little afraid. Remembering her manners, Sophia offered them a seat. To her surprise, instead of sitting on the other sofa, they both piled onto hers, bunching her up into a corner and forcing her to put her feet down on the carpet. With a silent look at one another, obviously deciding who would go first, Maddie began. "We had no idea about your mum. We just thought you didn't want to be friends anymore. Then when you started hanging with Dane McArdle, we just assumed you were dumping us. We're sorry." The apology was a collective one, meant sincerely twice over and Sophia looked at her old friends, a host of emotions clouding her view. When she said nothing, Heather chimed in, reiterating the apology and Sophia recognised a bone-tired ache in her soul and capitulated.

Forgiveness was a two-way street, offering healing on both sides. "It's ok," she said, so softly both girls leaned forward to hear her. "It's just been a really crap year."

Both girls did what girls do best, uniting in a messy group hug, offering comfort and solidarity as Sophia sniffed and cried on their designer clothes. Eventually, when the healing process was well underway, they went to the kitchen and raided the fridge and pantry for fizzy drinks and snacks. The girls hadn't heard about Dane, so Sophia cautiously filled them in, missing out any mention of Lou's pregnancy. She was aware as she thought about the lady vicar that she seemed to have gone from one extreme to the other - not telling anyone her mother was missing for months - to spilling her guts to everyone.

"That's radical," Heather said, swinging her long auburn hair over her shoulder. It was a new colour and very dramatic. In an extreme kind of way, it suited her. "I wish we could help."

"I know!" Maddie said, excitement taking hold. "Why don't we investigate? Oh my gosh, we could *so* do that."

"Where would we start?" Sophia asked, feeling tired at the thought of it. Maddie chewed a hang nail and worked on a plan.

Edgar was asleep on the bed, disturbed by the sound of the door opening. He thought for a moment Sal was stood over him and held his arms out to her. "You've come back," he said sleepily.

"Dad," his daughter whispered and he focussed his eyes to take in the vision of loveliness. Sophia stroked his hair back from his damp forehead. "Dad, I'm just nipping out with the girls. Heather's driving her mum's car. Yes, she's got her full licence and Maddie and me are going with her."

Edgar nodded slowly as he came to the surface more, his face a mask of sadness. Sophia sat down next to him, nudging him along so she could squeeze on. "Are you all right Dad?" she asked and stroked his fingers gently. He nodded and looked around the bedroom.

"Will you help me decorate in here?" The question surprised her and Sophia nodded. "It's too feminine now. It reminds me of how inadequate I am. I want something more...male."

"Oh, Dad. Don't be daft." His daughter kissed him on the side of the cheek, brushing her face against the Sunday stubble and wishing life was different for both of them. She remembered the words of the wise lady vicar and repeated them for his sake, "This too shall pass, Dad. It's for now, not forever. It'll all be ok. We'll look back this time next year and we'll have got through."

Edgar smiled and nodded as his pretty daughter left the room. She turned in the doorway and looked hard at her father. "You're not inadequate, Dad. You're a great father and I love you. You're the one who stayed for me. Don't forget that. I certainly won't."

A minute later he heard the front door slam and for the first time since his wife disappeared, Edgar's tears fell in torrents. It was silent crying, the very worst sort because it came from his soul and not his empty heart, already destroyed by loss and shame. He relived the nights of sitting up waiting for the sound of her key in the lock, poised and ready to tell her nothing mattered as long as she was back. It was a surprise to realise he no longer felt the same. Her disloyalty poisoned something deep inside him and he didn't think he would ever trust anyone again.

The crying seemed to last for hours, leaving Edgar exhausted and physically drained. But giving in was cathartic and he felt emotionally revitalised. It was as though he reached the bottom of himself and discovered it wasn't so bad down there. He touched ground zero in the pit of despair and began to float back up again, normality and sanity calling to him from the top of the well. It felt like miles away, but he knew he would get there.

Edgar stripped the bed and dismantled his bedroom, pulled up the carpet and exposing the rimu floorboards. He roared off in his SUV to the decorating superstore on Te Rapa with a spring in his step and a budding sense of optimism, his vibrant blue eyes twinkling for the first time in months.

Chapter Nine

"You knock!" Maddie urged Heather, stepping behind her at the last minute and cowering low in a display of cowardice.

"No! You knock!" Heather announced and dashed behind Sophia. They looked like a human whirlpool, swirling and churning around one another. The door opened suddenly and a little boy of about seven peeked out.

"What ya doin'?" he asked quizzically. He looked so adorable, the girls let out the kind of sigh females do in the face of extreme cuteness. He was like a very small, even blonder version of Darren, with the same extremely cheeky grin and look of feigned innocence.

"Is Darren in?" Sophia asked while Maddie and Heather let out combined 'aahs' in her ear. They looked like a shabby dance troupe with Sophia in front and the others lined up behind her, poking their heads out on either side.

The little boy turned on the spot, cupped his mouth in both tiny hands and yelled, "Darren!" like a displeased rugby coach bellowing from the sidelines.

"What? Stop yelling you stupid little..." Darren halted abruptly at the sight of the visitors, hastily cancelling his tirade. He stood in the doorway in jeans and a rumpled tee shirt which actually made him look marginally handsome. His face was one of disbelief and he swore without shame.

"Om er!" said the little boy, aghast. "Tellin' dad you said that!" The child darted off at a run but before his little bare feet could head off in the direction of trouble, Darren caught him by the shirt collar and gave him a look of pure menace.

The moment was intense and Sophia spoke into the awkwardness, her voice wobbling. "Er, we just came to look at the crime scene. We thought you lived around here and might like to come with us. Hope you don't mind."

"Oh, but..." Heather began and let out a squeak as Maddie kicked her in the ankle. Sophia turned and glared at them both. There was no need to explain how they searched the phone book for Darren's house number.

The small boy interrupted, "I don't mind you comin' round," he said happily. "I like girls. Can I sit on your knee?" He pointed at Heather, who gave an embarrassed smile and nodded. Sophia was impressed with her friends. After a shaky start, they were expertly playing the game. The little boy took Heather's hand and led her to a battered sofa outside the front of the porch. He waited for her to sit down and then plonked himself heavily on her legs. The others watched, feeling a little voyeuristic. The small boy was very forward. "I'm Toby," he said matter-of-factly, "will you be my girlfriend? My other one dumped me yesterday."

Heather made sympathetic noises, but her first mistake was in asking why.

"Well," the child launched into his saga, "I asked Miss if I could go to the toilet before sports but she said *no*. I got all the way to the top of the wall bars and couldn't help it. Peter Brockenhurst said it was like a shower and he'd never seen anything like it. I'm going to try and do it again next week and he's gonna shout 'tsunami' really loud and pay me five bucks. It was cool. And the teacher couldn't tell me off or nothing, cos I did ask her if I could go toilet."

Heather looked down at her knees in horror, hoping the child had showered and changed his shorts since Friday. There were no guarantees as he smiled mischievously up at her.

"Let's go for a walk," Darren jumped in helpfully and Heather looked relieved. "Not you!" he said, pointing to the small child, who screwed his face up in disappointment.

Heather extracted herself from underneath the boy and scurried out towards her friends, shooting looks of gratitude and hero worship at Darren. They walked down the street a short way and sat on the pavement opposite Dane's house. It looked a sorry mess with the crime scene tape fluttering in the breeze around it. They all stayed respectfully silent for a minute or two. Sophia hardened her resolve to get to the bottom of the murder, partly for Dane's sake and also to put an end to the things in her life making her miserable.

Darren pulled out his mobile phone and began pressing buttons. It became quickly apparent he was texting.

"Who are you talking to?" Maddie asked him and he smirked. "Asking Paul and Oliver to come over. They might like to hang with us."

"Not Oliver!" Sophia's tone was too sharp and she realised it the moment the sentence was out of her mouth. Darren looked at her quizzically. "Invite Paul that's fine," she said, more gently and he shrugged and wiped Oliver's name from the recipients' box.

"Don't you like Oliver?" Darren asked her and she shrugged. She couldn't possibly tell him they were using him. Sophia felt she could handle him and Paul, but Oliver was a far scarier prospect. In many ways he was a lot like Dane, silent and reserved. But he had a reputation for looking up skirts and down blouses at every opportunity and it would change the game plan somewhat, having to manage Oliver and not accidentally lead him on. "Come on, tell me," Darren pushed and Sophia knitted her brow.

"You'll tell people and I don't need the gossip," she said, keeping her voice low.

"Ohhhh!" Heather let out a long exclamation and widened her eyes. "You had problems with him last year, didn't you, Soph?"

Maddie slapped their mouthy friend on the leg and Heather bit her lip. "Sorry."

Darren narrowed his eyes and looked hard at Sophia. She sighed. "Fine! But I don't want it spreading round everywhere. Oliver asked me on a date last year and when I turned him down, he was spiteful and made some trouble for me. In the end, my older brother, Matt and some other Year 13's took him to one side and strongly suggested he leave me alone. It all stopped and it's been fine since."

Darren looked surprised. "I didn't know about that," he admitted. "He doesn't like being turned down. What kind of trouble?"

"Of the Sandie kind," Sophia sighed and her fingers strayed to her thigh, feeling the sensitive skin through her jeans.

"Oh." Darren bit his lip and then brightened. "Well the good news is he's never mentioned you so I guess he went off the idea." He looked longingly at Sophia. "So, with Dane banged up..." He didn't finish his sentence, but brushed her fingers gently with his own. Sophia's eyes flashed with irritation and she moved her hand out of reach. Darren shrugged and smiled.

They sat cross-legged on the pavement and chatted. It became quickly obvious the girls knew little about the group of boys whom Dane led and controlled for many years. "Yeah, we're always in trouble," Darren sniggered. "I guess we got used to Dane sorting it all out. He got fed up when Sandie's dad wouldn't help him with his stepdad. There was an almighty row and he left the group. The girls were gutted. We thought Sandie had it bad for him but it's funny because it wasn't actually her..."

"Nigel's a bit creepy," Heather interrupted. "I know he and Sandie got it on in the changing rooms once. That's kind of off-putting."

"Oh, really?" Darren said, as though he genuinely hadn't known. "What, the girls' ones?" He let out a hoot of laughter at Heather's nod of confirmation and rewarded her with a high five. Sophia worked hard at stilling her beating heart, spared the details of someone else's infatuation with Dane. Heather had accidentally stopped Darren confirming Sophia's suspicions about Lou's baby. Sophia focussed on a stray ant busying itself on the pavement and looked up to see Darren take a packet of cigarettes out of his jeans pocket with care and slip one into his mouth. He flicked the lighter expertly to set it burning. Remembering his manners, he offered them round. Sophia automatically declined and so did Heather, but Maddie's fingers hovered at the end of the packet. Darren smiled. "Try mine," he offered, taking a couple of good drags to make sure it was going.

Sophia felt both horrified at her friend and guilty at herself. "Maddie don't. You won't be able to stop. Edgar used to smoke. He smoked at home and especially in the car. He wouldn't let us have the back windows open when he did it and we felt like wasps under a glass, slowly suffocating."

"Has he stopped?" Darren sounded interested and paused in his cancerous activity.

Sophia nodded. "Yes. Matt got bronchitis once and was seriously ill in hospital. The doctor said passive smoking was partially responsible for his worsened condition and Edgar stopped. Just like that."

"Yeah that's what I'm gonna do," Darren interjected. He clicked his fingers. "I'm gonna stop, just like that."

Maddie took a tentative drag on the cigarette while Darren held it. Then she turned a nasty shade of green and started coughing her guts up. Darren laughed and banged her on the back. "I always wanted to try it," she gasped, trying to save face.

"You have to practice," Darren said laughing. "It's always bad at first."

"I don't think I want to practice," Maddie choked, recovering slowly and wiping tears from her eyes. Darren sat on his backside casually, knees bent and arms hanging down between. He chuckled as he carefully pulled a strand of tobacco off his tongue. When he looked sideways at Maddie, Sophia was alarmed to see her visibly melt under his gaze. She felt like an old fashioned chaperone, as though she should squeeze her bottom down between them to keep them apart.

"Blow backs are better," Darren said and took a long drag of the cigarette. Then before anyone could do anything, he leaned across and kissed Maddie on her open mouth, pushing the second-hand smoke into her lungs. Instead of choking, she looked as though she enjoyed it, jumping as Paul appeared and hurled himself down next to them on the pavement.

"Sweet sixteen and never been kissed," Paul said conversationally and Maddie blushed.

"That's not actually true, is it Madds?" Darren said with a slight smile on his face, looking at her from underneath his lashes. Poor Maddie went the colour of the red roses in Sophia's garden. Well, not exactly the same because their roses had dead bits on now her mother wasn't there to spray them anymore. But about that kind of red anyway. Maddie put her head down and Heather went on the offensive immediately.

"What's this?" she insisted. "How come I don't know anything about it?"

Maddie cringed a bit more and it was Paul who nonchalantly filled in the blanks for them. "Oh yeah. I remember. It was that Christmas disco in Year 10 wasn't it? You were holding that mistletoe and just swooped on her. Oliver said you were snogging her so long; he thought she might suffocate." He snorted with laughter, but Darren wasn't laughing. He gave Sophia an odd look. She kept her face passive, suddenly wondering if the kiss all those years ago was for her benefit. She remembered nothing of the incident, although it clearly had an impact on Maddie, whose face mottled as the blood tried to go back about its business in the rest of her body.

Getting no reaction whatsoever from Sophia, Darren decided to throw his energies into her friend. It was obvious Maddie was interested and so he cut his losses and went on a charm offensive with the impressionable teenager, completely unaware he was being played. He sidled closer to Maddie so their fingers touched, making it clear he was up for it. She bit her lower lip and gave him a coy smile. Heather and Sophia found it difficult to hide their shock at her behaviour.

"Were any of you here when the thing kicked off at Dane's house?" Sophia asked, pulling a face at Maddie to tell her to go easy. Both boys shook their heads.

"Mind you," Paul mused, "they were always arguing about something. Her fella used to take her clothes away so she couldn't leave. She'd hang the washing out in her panties, unless Dane was around. It didn't seem so bad then, probably because the old man took it out on him instead."

It made Sophia feel sick to her stomach to hear them speak so casually about family violence. The police tape flapped in the breeze like an accusation. Darren's interruption confounded her. "Dane killed him anyway. You said he did." He pointed at Sophia and her face registered shock.

"No I did not!"

"Yeah, you did," he maintained. "When I met you at the shops, I asked if Dane did them marks on your neck.

You said he hadn't but he sorted out who did. That meant he killed him, right?"

"No!" Sophia shook her head frantically. "That is definitely not what I meant!"

"Well, who done the marks then? His dad aye?"

"Yeah, but..." Her eyes widened. "Please tell me that you haven't told the cops I said that?"

Darren shrugged. "Don't make no difference to me. I'm glad the old bugger's dead. But no, I ain't telling the cops nothing. We don't snitch on our own round here." Distracted, he sidled closer to Maddie, shifting so their hips touched. Her arms were behind her, balancing her body as she stretched her legs out. Persistent, Darren casually crossed his arm over hers, indicating possession and it was raw and uncomfortable to watch. Maddie didn't flinch. Heather shot a look at Sophia, but the latter shrugged, having no idea what to do next.

"Come for a walk with me?" Darren asked Maddie and Sophia breathed out heavily. This wasn't part of the plan. There was no way she and Heather could allow the other girl to be separated from them. She stood up, indicating Heather should do the same and between them, they hauled Maddie off the ground. She seemed reluctant to leave.

Paul gave a cursory nod, clearly disappointed. "Hardly worth leaving the telly for," he muttered. "Thought we were gonna have some fun."

Heather kept a tight hold of Maddie's hand as Darren flicked his cigarette onto the road and put his hands on the girl's hips, pulling her into him. Their faces were only inches apart. He tipped forwards slightly and gave her a long lingering kiss. Maddie closed her eyes and horrified, Heather tugged her hand to pull her away. Maddie's lip gloss swiped right across Darren's lips and onto his cheek as she was yanked sideways and he left it there as he looked seductively at the unexpected object of his desire.

Paul smirked and shook his head, retrieving Darren's burning ciggie butt and taking a drag of it. "I miss Dane," he said to nobody in particular. "We were getting out of here." Of the group of boys, they were the only two quietly excelling in school, flying under the radar of hopelessness with good grades and a dream of escape.

"What do you mean?" Sophia asked him quietly.

He shrugged and drew on the cigarette again. "Ah, you know. Oliver will probably live round here until he swaps his dole for the state pension and so will the others. Darren will charm his way out, marry some rich woman with a high sex drive and make something of himself somewhere else."

Sophia saw him look sideways at Heather's long legs and grin at what he saw, his eyes widening in lust. "Maybe this is better than the crap Stallone movie we were watching."

The girls said their goodbyes, moving quickly along the street to where they parked the car a few blocks away. Maddie was silent, but Heather whinged continually. "I hope the car's still in one piece. Otherwise my mum will kill me!"

At the end of the road, Sophia looked back, hearing the sound of a freight train. It shook the ground like an earthquake and she wondered how people managed to live in such close proximity to the railway lines.

Something caught her eye and caused her to stop as she processed it. The last house on the street had a large bay window protruding out into the garden, surrounded by glass and net curtains. In her peripheral vision, Sophia saw the twitch of material as she turned. Something about it caused a curious feeling of déjà vu and she gripped her chest in confusion. "Ooh."

"Soph, what's wrong?" Heather stopped and looked at her with concern. She still held Maddie's hand, but the other girl seemed to be in cloud cuckoo land. "Do you think there was stuff in that cigarette?" Heather asked, jerking her head towards their friend.

Sophia smiled, remembering what it felt like when Dane kissed her, the smile fading on her lips as Lou jumped unbidden into her mind. If she allowed herself to think too much, it all became an insurmountable mess, so she focussed on one thing at a time.

"No. It was just a cigarette. I saw the packet. Take Madds to the car and drive around for a bit. I'm going to visit this house and see what I can find out. I seem to remember the curtains twitching as I ran away that day, but I'm not totally sure. I just need to knock and ask."

"The cops will have already done that," Heather said logically but Sophia shook her head.

"You heard what Darren said; they don't snitch on their own round here. Maybe they saw something and just told the cops they didn't. I need to try anyway."

At the mention of Darren, Maddie gave a little smile and looked momentarily interested. Heather hauled her off to the car, leaving Sophia in the street alone. The boys had long since loped off and she felt unnerved, standing outside the front of the 1930's wooden villa knocking on the front door. It opened slowly and the face of an elderly woman peeked out. "I'm not buying nothing!" she maintained forcefully and through the crack in the door, Sophia saw a tousled white head and a tiny body.

"I'm not selling," the girl called through the crack.

"You people always say that!" the old lady spat and Sophia's heart sank. She pressed herself closer to the wooden door.

"I visited the house along the street a few nights ago. My friend used to live there and I needed to pick something up for him. The man there...he...well, he hurt me and my friend came to help. As I ran away, I saw your curtains move and I just wondered if you saw anything that could help. Dane's been arrested..."

The door was flung back with vigour and the old lady was in front of Sophia in an instant. "Not lovely Dane?" she said, stepping into Sophia's personal space and peering up at her. "What's happened?"

The woman's frame was stooped and crooked, like a gnarled stick that underwent seasons of weather laid on the damp ground. She seized Sophia's hand and pulled her into the house behind her, shutting the door and shuffling down a long hallway. At the back of the house, she opened the door into a beautiful sunlit room. An elderly man lay in a hospital bed hooked up to an oxygen kit, his breathing laboured and loud, adding to the hiss of the cylinder. Still holding Sophia's hand, the woman shuffled over to the man and told him in a loud voice, "I've just got a visitor, Clive. I'll come and give you dinner very soon, my love."

Then she turned and led the girl all the way back down the hallway to the room at the street end of the house. Sophia hadn't expected it to be the kitchen, surprised by the size of the room and the homeliness of it.

Pale blue wooden units surrounded the walls, old and tired but adding to the cosiness of the space. A huge kitchen table graced the centre and the lady flapped at it with her hand. "Sit down, sit down." She filled an old fashioned gas kettle and sat it on the rings of a hob. She fiddled around making a pot of tea and setting out cups, as though she hadn't entertained a decent visitor for a long time. The milk tasted a little sour, but Sophia didn't want to offend the woman by rejecting her hospitality. She sipped the drink and prayed protection over her stomach.

"What's your name?" the old lady asked, finally sitting down opposite the teenager.

"Sophia," she replied and the woman nodded.

"Ah yes, Dane mentioned you often. I told him just to go ahead and ask you on a date. He never would though. He's like my Clive. It took him months to pluck up the courage to ask me to the local tea dance." She laughed indulgently, her face dropping suddenly, "We fell in love just as he went off to war. He came back quite smashed up. It's the cancer that's got him now though. That's worse than anything they did to him in Europe. He recovered from that, but he won't get better now, not from this."

Sophia bit her bottom lip, as sadness pervaded. It seemed that all around her nowadays was the grey hallmark of its fingers, spreading into every area of her life.

"Don't be sad for me," the woman chided her. "We've had more than seventy years together. I'm ninety-three this year." She sipped her tea from a delicate china mug with shaking hands. "So tell me about Dane. What's going on with him? Oh, and call me Hettie. Dane does.

Sophia laid out the whole sorry saga and Hettie listened intently. "That's not right," she said eventually.

"I saw you arrive. I always notice new people here, out of that window." She pointed to the bay window facing the street like an eye.

"Would you mind," Sophia asked, "if I record what you say on my phone?" She pulled out her mobile. "I'm scared of forgetting things and I think you might know something important. But I probably won't know it until after you've said it."

The old lady nodded and smiled. "Gee, I feel important. Like a proper interview then. Like on 'Campbell Live' or something." The thought seemed to tickle her greatly, but she went on with her story, "I spend most of my day in here, or down with Clive. The district nurse was due, so I watched out of the window for her. I can't hear the door if I'm down with Clive because of the oxygen hissing and my ears aren't so sharp anymore. I saw you go across there and go in. I've got a good view from the side window here. Her that lives there answered the door in her knickers as always. I was surprised because you looked like such a nice girl, too nice to be buying their drugs. When you went in I made a pot of tea and put the radio on, but I saw Dane arrive and knew there would be trouble. I'm glad he took the little kids away."

Hettie sipped her tea through dry lips cracked with age. "They stayed here once you know, while Child Services tried to find somewhere for them to go in a hurry. They were angels, so silent I hardly knew they were here and the wee boy was little more than a baby. He didn't make a sound. It was unnatural. But Dane knows what it's like with Clive now and I wouldn't cope with them all here. Dane helps me move him, see. When he gets home from work, often he'll come in and help me turn him over. The nurse says it's a miracle Clive doesn't have more bed sores, but that's because of Dane. He mows my grass too. He's a godsend is that boy. Never takes no money, just uses Clive's old mower and leaves it nice and clean. Sometimes he brings me the plants from his work that the boss says are no good. I make them all better in the greenhouse out back. Clive used to love his greenhouse."

Hettie sighed as her mind wandered off to happier times and Sophia struggled to bring her back. "Why did you think there would be trouble when Dane arrived?" she asked, worrying about the answer, but knowing the cops were bound to ask it too. She needed to be prepared for what came next in case it was damning.

"Because that man hated Dane. He's taken him out the front and hit him many times. My neighbour, Eric, he was a gunner in the war and he pulled the stepfather off him once. Eric's dead now; God rest his soul, but he was so angry about it. 'You don't treat kids like that,' he said to him and the man just laughed in his face. I don't know why she married him, her in her knickers. They were a nice family until then, even without a husband. She didn't need that jailbird."

"Tell me about that night?" Sophia asked gently.

"Well, Dane tore in and then you came out and ran to the end of the street. I could see that you were crying and hurt, but by the time I opened the door, you were gone around the corner. Dane came running out after you almost straight away and then another man appeared. He was naked from the waist up and he grabbed the boy. I hadn't seen him before. Dirty looking fella."

Hettie shifted in her seat and cocked her head like a small bird at a faint noise, halting her storytelling so she could listen. Satisfied it wasn't a problem with Clive, she relaxed. "He hit Dane over the back of the head with a metal thing – like one of the legs from them garage shelves. The boy stopped dead and put his hand up to his head and then his stepdad appeared and smacked him straight in the face. He went down like a stone and didn't seem to be moving. Then the guy got on top of him and started laying into him while he was down. We don't have a telephone, you see, so I couldn't call for help. But I got my shoes on – it took me a bit because I can't bend down properly – but when I got to the door, Dane was walking to his car. The step dad and the other man stood on the grass shouting at him. I didn't see his mother then. Maybe she went to put some pants on." Hettie giggled naughtily and then looked guilty. "Well, why would you stand there in your knickers when your husband's got guests?"

Sophia smiled, but hope burgeoned in her heart like a budding flower. "So you're sure when Dane got into his car and left the street, his stepfather was alive and well?"

"Oh yes. Definitely. That's why I'm surprised you're saying they've arrested him."

"Did you see him come back, Dane I mean?" Sophia asked, desperate to account for that rogue half hour which Dane hadn't yet explained.

To her disappointment, Hettie couldn't swear that he didn't return later. "The district nurse arrived shortly after and she always stays for a cup of something with me. It wasn't until she was leaving that all the police cars turned up, making a noise and upsetting my Clive. They did call yesterday, some young pup that didn't look old enough to be out of school, let alone wearing a policeman's uniform. I just told him to go away. They wouldn't help us when the druggies were hanging around and all the young families moved out of the street. So I didn't feel minded to help them in return. I should have though. I didn't know Dane needed my help. Please tell him I'm sorry, won't you, love?"

Sophia nodded and asked her gently, "My Uncle Bob is trying to help Dane. He's a lawyer and Dane's being transferred from the hospital to the police station tomorrow for questioning. Can I tell Uncle Bob to call on you?"

Hettie nodded. "All right, dear. But tell him to bring some Scottish shortbread from the English Shop. The one with the red packet. Dane sometimes brings us some, but he hasn't done it for a few weeks, not since that evil man turned up again."

Hettie smiled and her top row of false teeth dropped down onto the bottom set with a clack. It was slightly alarming, but Sophia managed to ignore it, turning her attention to the mobile phone with its precious recording. She left the house eventually, after helping the old lady to lift and turn the man in the bed to alleviate the pressure on his spine. He groaned as they shifted him, but Hettie prattled on as though nothing was wrong and it broke Sophia's tender heart to see the loyalty and devotion. It made her dwell on Edgar and Sal and depression shrouded her as she reached Heather's car.

Chapter Ten

"You were ages!" the girls whinged. "We thought you'd been kidnapped!"

"My hair's gone all frizzled in the heat!" Maddie wittered.

Sophia told them the bare bones of her successful mission and they were elated; high fiving each other and feeling as smart as regular women detectives. Sophia got Heather to drive her round to the Robertson's house and leave her there. Bob welcomed her with hugs and Ellen with kisses, but neither were impressed with her, once she told them her news. In fact, Bob was livid. "You bloody well did what?"

"Now steady on, Bob. Remember your blood pressure," Ellen interjected. "She's only done what you would have."

"It's a police investigation!" he shouted and Ellen flapped her arms at him.

"And she's worked out what they couldn't. She won't go back there, will you, Soph?"

"Well, I was hoping to come back and interview Hettie with you…"

At the sight of Bob going a horrid shade of puce, Sophia decided perhaps home was a better place for her. Bob confiscated her phone, wrote down Hettie's address and the instruction about the shortbread and drove her home.

At the house, Edgar's SUV was parked on the driveway, which was unusual and another car parked behind it. Sophia stared at it as she and Bob went up the front steps. "I've seen that car somewhere before," she mused. Bob put his fingers firmly into the centre of her back and pushed her up to the front door.

As the door clicked shut behind them, two little bodies hurled themselves at the girl's legs.

SOPHIA'S DILEMMA 143

"Soph!" Maisie squealed, demanding to be picked up, while William hugged her thighs and kissed the front of her jeans.

"Oh, thank God!" Sophia sighed loudly and saw the odd look Bob gave her. She was thrilled to see Dane's brother and sister but even more pleased to be spared the double telling-off Bob planned to act out alongside Edgar.

"Luff you, Soph," Will whispered and snuggled into Sophia's legs. She sank down onto the steps so she could hold them and enjoy their fragile bodies and childish scent. They reminded her of Dane and happier times.

Marie and Carl sat in the family room with glasses of cold water and Edgar wore very old clothes covered in splashes of paint. Sophia looked at him curiously. Edgar greeted Bob warmly and introduced him to the children's foster carers. Sophia was grateful Bob didn't just launch into her catalogue of errors, but the look he gave her told her she was going to get it later.

"We haven't met," Marie said, shaking Sophia's hand, "but the children talk about you all the time."

Sophia's mind took her back to the awful night a few weeks ago, when Dane had arrived in the early hours, injured and trailing his tiny responsibilities.

"Yes," she smiled sadly. "They came here a few weeks ago when...well, when it all went wrong at their place. They stayed overnight and disappeared the next day."

Sophia sat on the floor with a child on each knee, their little arms tangled around her neck. They had a little whispered spat about who loved her most, but in the end agreed that it was probably Dane and shut up.

Edgar's smile encompassed Bob and Sophia as he announced, "Carl and Marie can account for Dane's whereabouts during that missing half an hour the other night. He turned up at their place, covered in cuts and looking sick. He wanted to see the kids."

Carl looked suddenly very guilty. "I could see he'd been in a fight and wanted to help him get cleaned up before they saw him. They've just started to settle and I didn't think it was helpful for them to see him bleeding. He didn't seem quite right; he kept repeating himself. I took him into the lounge and sat him down so I could go and get some first aid supplies from the kitchen. I was only gone for a few seconds but when I got back, he wasn't there. The ranch slider was open and I heard his car start. I couldn't catch him and we haven't seen him since. We got worried and tried all the numbers we had, but couldn't reach him. I know we didn't meet, but we picked the children up from this house a few weeks ago. We thought we'd try here. We've been a couple of times, but figured a Sunday evening was probably the best time to catch anyone in."

Sophia cuddled the little bodies to her firmly, knowing in part, the nightmare was over. She loved their tiny arms and legs and how strong their hold on her was. They were so loyal and sweet, despite all the harm adults in their life had caused. Smelling the strong washing powder scent on William's clothes made her want to cry, making an imprint of the children for her memories, figuring she probably wouldn't see them again. Sophia concentrated on the familiar ache in the healing scar on her thigh as William's bony bottom compressed it.

She used it to distract herself from the sadness inside. *Mission accomplished*. She did it. She salvaged Dane's job for him, proved he didn't kill his stepdad and ensured he wouldn't go to prison.

Bob took Sophia's mobile phone to the police station with Carl, to meet the detective handling the murder enquiry. Then he went to see Hettie. Maria took the little children home. They hugged and kissed Sophia with genuine affection. "Luff you heaps and heaps, Soph. When can we see you again?"

"Oh, soon guys," she sniffed, dangerously close to breaking. As Edgar shut the door after their departure, he didn't expect his daughter to break down into floods of tears.

"I thought you'd be happy, sweetheart," he said gently into her hair. "I guess it's just the stress of it all."

But it wasn't. It was the end of something very wonderful and Sophia didn't want to face it. She should have rung Maddie and Heather with the good news; knowing they would celebrate how their sleuthing paid off, but she couldn't quite bring herself to. She needed to finish with Dane, but wasn't yet sure how to do it. Writing a note was the coward's way out, although maybe things would have been different if Sally at least dignified Edgar with one.

To her dismay, a knock on the door a few hours later admitted an elated Bob, closely followed by the tall figure of Dane. Sophia knew she went immediately red and cursed her pale skin for betraying her. Dane seemed awkward and still in pain and Bob informed them he had discharged himself as soon as the handcuffs were removed.

"Would it be alright if he stayed here, just for tonight?" Bob asked Edgar and Sophia cringed visibly.

SOPHIA'S DILEMMA

She knew Dane saw, his dark eyebrows knitting just slightly at her reaction and she worked hard to keep her face neutral. "You're jolly quiet, Miss Armitage, I must say!" Bob said to her and she looked down at the carpet anxiously, finding Dane's eyes on her as she looked up again. The situation was agonising.

The sound of a key rattling around in the front door sent Edgar out into the hallway leaving the two teenagers, the jubilant and oblivious lawyer and one hell of an atmosphere. Running footsteps came down the hall to the family room and Sophia's mother burst in, closely followed by Edgar. She faltered slightly as she saw her old employer, at least having the decency to look ashamed. Dane had a double take at the older version of Sophia, dressed in neat slacks with a lacy summer top that fitted where it touched. "What the hell's going on with my daughter?" she said accusingly, looking straight at Edgar. "You told me she wasn't the one stabbed at school. Now I find out that she *was*. And what's this about a criminal boyfriend?"

Edgar's face was impassive and feeling suddenly in the way; Bob reached down from his great height and kissed Sophia gently on the cheek. Raising his eyebrows, he said in a low voice, "We can have a little chat about personal safety and risk taking, another time."

He shook hands warmly with Dane and Edgar and behaved as though Sally hadn't just burst into the room, leaving without looking in her direction. It didn't faze her in the slightest. "Is anyone going to explain?" she demanded and Edgar shrugged and went into the kitchen to boil the kettle, for a drink he didn't want. He wasn't about to stand and argue with the vitriolic woman.

Sal turned to look at her daughter, her eyes softening and she modified her tone. "Soph, are you ok?"

Am I ok? Sophia decided the answer was probably *no*. Right then, she was far from ok. But she nodded anyway, wanting the moment to be over and her mother to go back to wherever she came from.

Spotting Dane propping himself up against the television cabinet, looking like he badly wanted to sit down but didn't feel it was appropriate, Sally pointed a perfectly manicured finger at him. "Please tell me this is *not* the criminal boyfriend? And please tell me he isn't staying here with my sixteen-year-old daughter?"

Something snapped inside Sophia. She wondered if it began with the appearance of a woman she hadn't seen for almost three months, a woman who was *meant* to feel something for her, but clearly didn't. Or perhaps the crater in her heart split open with the use of the word, 'boyfriend.' The cyclone inside welled up with such violence it took even her by surprise and she felt like a detached spectator, watching herself get right into her mother's personal space and shout into her face. "He isn't my boyfriend! He's having a baby with someone else! You don't have any rights here! Leave Dad alone and stay away from me! I have nothing else left for you to take!"

Then she ran, fresh energy coursing through her veins, mixing with the adrenaline and endorphins as Sophia pounded down the stairs and flung open the front door. She had no idea where she was going, but ran anyway. The tiny bits of metal which became detached from the pavement in the extreme heat, bit and stabbed into her bare feet as she blindly hurtled down the alleyway at the end of the street. Discovery Park opened up in front of her and she pelted across the grass, feeling a wonderful freedom.

Halfway across, her brain finally got her attention and she slumped down in the middle of a soccer pitch. The paddock was infested with onehunga weed and the prickles pushed their way into the soles of her feet, embedding themselves and causing her pain sensors to object. She didn't know whether to laugh or cry. "It's like everything else in my life!" she yelled. "It looks good from a distance, but when you get up close it's *irreparably broken!*"

The vast area of green was deserted. Nobody heard or cared. Sophia sat and picked the prickles out of her feet, hoping nobody came looking for her. "Especially *her!*" she muttered, knowing a visit from her mother would finish her off. At least they all knew how she felt now. With any luck, by the time she composed herself enough to get home again, there would only be good old Edgar left to pick up the pieces and glue her together. Sophia pulled the last prickle out and hobbled over to the play park, feeling grateful for the small mercy of privacy. The lady-vicar's words came back to her, "*This too shall pass,*" bringing her distant hope.

"Sophia Armitage, you've survived worse," she told herself, acknowledging the truth with sadness. She plonked herself on the swings, relishing the temporary freedom being high in the air brought and closing her eyes, she dreamed of happier times back when her family was whole and her parents were still the people she believed them to be. After a stomach churning swing, Sophia knew she needed to stop and re-enter the real world. It came to her like a bitter blow; she couldn't aimlessly swing here for the rest of her life and then just die. More's the pity.

The surface under the swing held the day's heat and felt sore on Sophia's bare feet when she tried to stop. She kept her eyes closed and coasted to a steady halt, each swing bringing her back under the control of gravity. She wondered how long it would take for Dane to find somewhere else to go and her mother to return to her love nest. She opened her eyes, deciding to wait for another half an hour just to make sure.

A dark movement in her peripheral vision made Sophia jump and she whipped her head round. Dane sat on the swing next to her. His dark hair hung in his eyes, his head lowered to face the ground. His left hand clutched the chain of the swing, but his other gripped his damaged ribs. Sophia stopped her swing and felt a familiar sensation as her brain dried up and left her no words to speak. *Mind blank*.

Sophia bit her lip and stood on the superheated surface with a wince of pain. She felt Dane's stare on the side of her face and gulped. It was hard not to turn and acknowledge him. She promised herself she would never let a guy get to her like this again, never give someone else the right to break her like Sal destroyed Edgar. Dane's blue eyes burned in her cheek and eventually she succumbed and peeked. Everything about him looked ill, his colour, his posture and the dampness of his hair where it met his forehead. But his eyes were steady and powerful, like intense blue pools of water. They were the colour of the icy lahar at the top of Mount Ruapehu, almost a perfect reflection of the bright summer sky. His dark lashes blinked and Sophia sighed. It was important to do this right and she was brought up to be nice. "I don't think we should see each other anymore...like this," she said, her voice steady but her heart shattering like a crystal vase. She wafted her hand to take in the play park, the soccer pitches and the endless weed-infested grass.

"Like this...as in, on children's apparatus." Dane didn't smile.

"No! Like this, as in...my...boyfriend." Even saying the word seemed to cut like a knife, irritation budding in Sophia's tone.

"So I gathered," Dane replied. "Can I ask why?"

She looked at him with astonishment. "Because of the baby you're having with Lou! I'm not getting in the middle of that."

Dane shook his head to clear it, moving his hand from his ribs to rub his eyes and back again. "I'm just not getting this," he said, sounding desperate. Sophia resented having to explain it to him. She wanted to leave him sitting there pathetically on a child's swing and go home, but fear of him falling off, dictated she stay. It was a bit pointless getting the cops off his back only to leave him to die in a kiddie's playground.

"Lou is pregnant!" Sophia gritted her teeth, stilting her sentence. "I heard her say it was yours and you wouldn't take responsibility. I don't want to be involved. I feel...confused."

"*You* feel confused! Welcome to the club!"

"Oh my gosh! So, you're still denying it? Poor Lou."

"Oliver!" Dane gasped as he tried to sit up. "Oliver got Lou pregnant, not me. Get your facts straight!"

Sophia shook her head. "I heard her say..."

What actually did she hear? Sophia tried to conjure up the awful scene in the toilet. It shouldn't have been hard; she went over and over it many times since. But as she replayed the chance conversation, the words rearranged themselves unhelpfully in Sophia's head and she realised with horror; Lou said nothing of the kind. She never said Dane's name.

"Lou wouldn't say it's mine, because it's not!" Dane said, emitting a tight, awful cough. "So at what point did you jump to your damning little conclusion?" His voice held the sneer Sophia heard him use on other people and it chipped away at the ice over her heart.

"She said the father wasn't interested because he liked someone else. Then she wished Sandie had chopped that person's leg off." Sophia gulped.

"Right!" Dane hauled himself up using the swing chain and the seat jerked and hit him in the butt. His eyes flashed dangerously from inside a pain wracked face. "Well, thanks for that. Thanks for coming to me first with your imaginative speculation...oh, you didn't." He shook his head at her, even the slight action paling his colour further.

The jigsaw pieces fell into place quickly as Sophia recalled the 'little chat' Matt and his mates had with Oliver last year. Remorse rode her like a rodeo bronc, relentlessly digging in its heels and making her squirm.

"But Darren hinted at it too. He said it wasn't just Sandie that had the hots for you. I assumed it was Lou."

"It was *Janine!*" Dane spat. "And just so you know, Janine really is my cousin. Our junkie, alcoholic mothers are sisters, so it was hardly likely to happen, was it? Why unite two defective sides of the same family? Besides the very obvious fact that I always fancied *you*, so it was pointless. They all knew that!"

Sophia let out a heavy sigh and hung her head.

"So let me get this straight," Dane said, fixing his flashing eyes on her face. His breath came in short pants and he gripped his side. "You were one of the few people who *didn't* believe I killed my stepdad and told me you loved me while I was handcuffed to the bed. Yet you would so easily believe I could knock someone up and just leave them to deal with it alone?" He shook his head sadly. "You're not the person I thought you were. *Fine.* We're done, Soph. As soon as I can get across there, I'll be out of your life for good!"

Dane's hand waved towards the alleyway onto Sophia's street as his chosen direction, before pitching forward. His butt rested back on the swing seat and he coughed again. Blood spattered onto the floor and Sophia leapt in terror. "What can I do? Dane, you're bleeding!" She desperately wanted to touch him, her hand reaching out to stroke his hair but Dane's recoil was enough to warn her off. "I'll get help," she squeaked. "But Uncle Bob took my phone to the cops. I'll have to run home." She hovered, unsure of herself.

Dane said nothing, coughing up more spray onto the ground. Sophia took off running, skirting the spiteful grass and pounding her sore feet over yet more stones and grit. At the front door, she hammered until Edgar answered it. "It's open!" he greeted her crossly. "It's like a bloody motorway in here anyway...Soph? What's happened?"

Her ashen face crumpled in misery and Edgar sighed and held his daughter tightly, her feet bleeding into the bristly door mat.

Edgar drove the SUV round to the park and retrieved Dane with great difficulty. The teenager refused to go back to the hospital.

"Fine!" Edgar retorted in annoyance. "But don't die in my son's bloody bed or I'll kill you!"

Dane rolled his eyes and leaned on the man's arm, pushing Sophia's helping hand away. She sat in the back of the car broken by Dane's rejection, knowing she deserved it.

Edgar put him to bed in Matt's old room and even though he was only the other side of the wall and she didn't sleep a wink, Sophia neither heard nor saw Dane again that night.

Chapter Eleven

"I've taken the day off to look after Dane, but I'll have your new car fetched home by one of the mechanics after it's been serviced and warranted," Edgar said, popping his head round Sophia's door as she got ready for school.

She smiled and tried to look happy, but her heart wasn't in it. "Thanks, Dad."

Things should have been great at school, apart from Lou puking all over the eyeballs she was dissecting in biology and the teacher having to clear the classroom. The friendship with Maddie and Heather restarted as though there hadn't been a painful hiatus and it was comforting for Sophia to achieve a tiny portion of normality in her tumultuous life.

Darren developed a full-on crush for Maddie, behaving like a paper wasp, always coming at her from whichever direction they went. "Hey, gorgeous," he crooned, kissing her wetly outside the science block. He eyed Sophia sideways and she smiled graciously and released him from her emotionally. He winked and put his energies into making Maddie flush red. He was kind of sweet and made Sophia smile more than cringe.

Paul hung around as well, making a play for Heather, who made a great show of resisting. They chatted on the way to English. "Look, I'll bow out gracefully when Dane comes back and you can all hang together," Sophia offered.

"You broke up?" Heather looked appalled. "After proving he didn't do it and working his job for him! What a creep!"

"No," Sophia defended Dane. "It's fine. It's mutual. It was never going to work. We're too different."

"That sucks!" Paul commented. "He's liked you since Year 9. He tried to keep the girls away from you and gave Oliver a slap last year for pushing you around. Are you sure you got this right?"

"Oh, yes! Definitely," Sophia breathed, swallowing the choking sensation in her throat.

"Poor baby." Heather put her arm around her friend and squeezed. "Well, you're not going anywhere so he'll have to get used to it."

Sophia smiled and cringed, knowing she wouldn't be able to hang around someone she had wronged so badly. Besides, Dane hated her.

She decided she didn't care anymore. The solid things in life were never what she thought they were, crashing down around her ears and doing so much damage – more than she ever thought possible. Friends, parents – *boyfriends*.

Edgar's SUV was on the driveway, but Sophia's new car wasn't yet. A note in the kitchen said he was taking the mechanic back to the garage and would fill it up for her, so they could have a little test drive that evening. She smiled at the effort Edgar was making and looked forward to it, stroking the funny little smiley face her father drew on the notepaper.

She wandered down the hallway whistling under her breath and bumped into Dane coming out of the bathroom, still wet from the shower. He groaned as the impact shook every aching part of him and he closed his eyes and leaned against the wall for a moment. The white gauze over his chest wound oozed red stuff and his rib cage displayed most of the colours of the rainbow. His jeans hung below his striped boxer shorts, revealing his massive weight loss recently through stress and injury.

"Sorry," Sophia said, waiting for him to show he was all right before moving on.

"It's fine." He spoke through gritted teeth and Sophia shrugged and turned to leave, trying not to focus on Dane's sculpted chest and stomach, or respond to the sinking feeling in the pit of her stomach.

"Wait!" He reached for Sophia's wrist and she dragged it away, waving arrogantly behind her as she walked down the corridor. "Bloody women!" Dane exclaimed and followed her. Sophia heard his breath coming in quick rasps as he covered the short distance between them in seconds. She felt the inexplicable urge to run, squealing as Dane's tanned arm blocked her route into the bedroom. His forearm rested against the doorframe next to her face, his height towering over her like a bridge. His heady proximity made her close her eyes and fight her attraction.

"I got a call from Harold," Dane said, flexing his arm muscles as Sophia pushed against it. "Don't walk away from me, Soph." His voice held warning, but when she looked into his face, his eyes sparkled and danced with the thrill of the chase. She sighed like an insolent child and rolled her eyes. Dane smirked.

"If you thought so badly of me, why did you go to all that trouble? You've been doing my job for me. A bit too well, by Harold's account!" He reached out and fingered a curly lock of Sophia's hair and she shivered. Dane's eyes became sultry and he moved his hand up to her neck.

Sophia gave a little shrug, ignoring the disturbing sensations in the pit of her stomach. "Because," she said simply. *This too shall pass*.

"And apparently, I've been shortlisted for a scholarship I never even applied for."

"Oh crap! The cops took your passport and birth certificate. They came for it on Saturday as evidence. They made Dad hand it over."

Sophia's emotions rocked in her chest, making her feel seasick. She pushed at Dane's arm and considered kicking him in the shins. His blue eyes flashed with recognition and she blushed, caught contemplating violence against someone already weakened. "I would!" she threatened, danger in her eyes. "But my feet are still very sore and you're not worth it!"

"Soph," Dane said softly, his voice barely above a whisper, "let's stop this, please?"

She gritted her teeth and tried to think of something else. *Her new car. Her bright red, shiny new car, which was about to arrive any second now and then she would go driving and then...*

The thought died in her brain as he reeled her in, gently pulling at her waist until he managed to enfold Sophia's stiff body completely in his arms. He smelled of shower gel and shampoo and his skin was soft and damp. "I'm sorry," he whispered as he kissed her cheek and she felt the wet towel in his hand, seeping water through the back of her school blouse. "I shouldn't have got mad. I can see how it looked."

Dane's lips settled fully on hers and Sophia let out a sigh of resignation, enfolding herself in his familiar kisses and enjoying the plummeting sensations as her heart plunged into her knees. Dane's tongue probed her mouth gently and he dropped the towel, breathing through his nose as their passion heightened. Sophia felt hard muscle either side of his spine and caressed the tanned skin with tentative fingers, feeling Dane shiver with anticipation as he deepened the kiss.

The hall door opened with a loud bang, making them both jump. Edgar and Bob stood framed in the doorway. Edgar jangled a set of car keys in his fingers, his eyebrows raised in question and his disciplinarian's face already in position.

Bob had an exceedingly smug look on his face and to Sophia's surprise, laughed. "And that," he announced splendidly, as though summing up his case to a spellbound jury and pointing at Dane, "is exactly why this young man is coming to live with me!"

Epilogue

Extract from an article in the local newspaper dated two days later.

'Tonight, Police and Fire Investigators are looking into a house fire in the suburb of Fairview which destroyed a one storey dwelling and killed its single occupant. The house next to the railway line was boarded up and cordoned off by police, following a murder at the same address last Thursday night. Police had concluded their forensic examination of the property and it was sealed pending decontamination.

Police allege the house had been used as a 'P' lab over recent weeks. It is believed the deceased male entered the property, having been a former resident. He had been implicated in the death of Peter Hugh Marton at the property, but police were still pursuing their enquiries. A local source who declined to be named, has told this newspaper both men were engaged in the manufacture and distribution of pseudoephedrine and had a volatile relationship, which often resulted in physical fights.

Hettie Lassiter, 93, has lived in the street for sixty years with her husband, Clive 91. "I don't think I've seen this much excitement in the street before. But me and my Clive aren't surprised at how it's all ended. I'm just sorry for the kiddies who lived there. Hopefully now they can go and make good lives for themselves someplace else. They always deserved better than that."

Fire Investigators say initial findings indicate the likelihood that the occupant fell asleep with a lighted cigarette in the kitchen area of the house, previously used as the clandestine "P"-lab. The presence on fittings of the highly flammable chemical residue from the cooking process led to the explosion.

The deceased cannot be named until immediate family have been located. The coroner is expected to record his verdict at a hearing next month.'

Please help me?

It would mean the world to me if you would leave a review for this story.
I can't manage without them and I value your opinion.
You can do this by going to my website ktbowes.com or by emailing me directly at admin@ktbowes.com
I would be very grateful.
Definitely get in touch when you've written a review.
Please give me the chance to say thank you.

Bonus chapter

Are you desperate for a taste of the next story?
Read on...
A Trail of Lies is set in the same school, but looks at the issues surrounding another couple, Callister Rhodes and Declan Harris.
If you're hooked on Dane and Sophia, feel free to skip to Book 4 *Gone Phishing*.
But Callister and Declan will be there too, so you may as well get to know them first.
Keep reading.

A Trail of Lies

The dull razor blade tinkled out onto the shower tray, glinting up at her beneath the cascading water. Calli stood holding the redundant plastic casing of her razor, her olive face scowling in irritation at the implement's betrayal. What else could go wrong today?

The teenager looked down at her tanned calves as the shower spray pounded the back of her willowy neck. They didn't look too hairy; she could probably get away with it as long as they didn't have assembly. Anyone sitting on the assembly hall floor close to her would notice the small protrusions of downy hair sneaking out of her pores. Calli considered shouting for her mother, instantly rejecting the thought. The new razors were in the hall cupboard. Marcia would yell at her, especially while she was trying to get ready for work and sort the little kids out.

Calli let the soap run from her body unhindered. She smoothed conditioner into her unruly, black curls and let it stay there, the wetness touching the bottom of her back uncomfortably. She turned off the shower even as the frantic knocking sounded on the bathroom door. "Hurry up, Calli, I've got netball practice at seven thirty! If I'm not there on time, the coach will make me sit out of the first quarter on Saturday. Come out, or I'll get Mum!"

Exasperated, Calli snatched up the errant razor blade and gingerly picked her way out of the slippery shower. Winding her towel around her so she could unlock the bathroom door and admit her desperate, whining sister, she felt the blade's sharp point slip underneath the skin of her index finger and winced. She couldn't leave it in the bathroom bin in case Jase found it. She wouldn't put it past her baby brother to do some serious damage to himself, out of boyish curiosity. "There!" she said rudely to the skinny blonde girl who bounced up and down on the balls of her feet outside the bathroom in a thin, cotton nightdress. "Try to get up on time next week."

Calli was almost at her bedroom door when her sister let out a piercing screech, "Mum! Callister's been using my shower gel!"

Calli rolled her appealing blue eyes and slammed her door on the ensuing scene, currently unfolding on the landing outside the bathroom. The razor blade produced a small nick that was painful, but not life-threatening. It bled a little as the sixteen year old got dressed in her school uniform, tartan skirt and white blouse. She pulled her damp curls back into a ponytail and pouted lips that rarely exhibited their fullness in a smile. Of all of her siblings, Calli was the only one who looked like her Samoan father. Raven haired and olive skinned like Simon, the others were blonde; blue eyed, sylphlike carbon copies of Marcia, their mother. It always made Calli feel like an outsider, her dark ringlets betraying her even when the other children were white blonde from the sunshine. She once heard an old lady in the park ask her mother if she was adopted. Calli would have loved to have been blonde, with easy-to-manage poker straight hair. She might have fitted in better.

Sighing, the girl straightened her school tie and slipped on the horrid black roman sandals that were part of the school issue uniform. Turning away from the mirror after a cursory check, she refused to look at herself again. There was no point. It changed nothing.

"Calli-Walli!"

The steady knocking came from somewhere near the bottom half of the bedroom door. With an exasperated shake of her head; Calli wrenched it open to find her tiny brother standing there, his shorts on backwards and his shirt buttoned up at the wrong intervals so his small chest resembled a rolling seascape. "Help me?" he beseeched her and pulled a cute face.

"Good boy for knocking, Jase," she told him, pulling him into the room so she could sit on the edge of the bed and deal with his haphazard dressing.

"I'm a good boy," he repeated as his older sister redid his buttons and persuaded him to step out of his shorts and back in again.

"You've almost finished a whole term at big school," Calli said softly, stroking his white blonde hair back from his forehead. He nodded, his face innocently proud, before snuggling in for a cuddle, his five year old hands reaching around his sister's slender waist for a moment.

"Can I have my Easter egg now?" he asked with a cheeky grin and Calli smiled. "Good Friday is the day after tomorrow, so only four more sleeps to go."

Jase nodded, understanding completely, but knowing with that childish optimism it was worth a try. "Will you do my buckles please?" he asked her, looking up with his bright blue eyes. "Mummy does them too tight and it hurts me."

Calli nodded and smiled as he skipped off to get them, singing to himself. She loved her brothers, especially Jase, but clashed unbearably with eight year old Sadie. Her younger sister was a lot like Marcia. Calli and her mother both regularly sparked like an electrical storm, frequently causing significant damage to their surroundings. It was of little surprise that from the start, Calli turned her nose up at the blonde baby girl Marcia proudly presented. The fireworks began as soon as Sadie was able to let out that irritating whine.

"Get breakfast, Calli!" Marcia's blonde head popped through the open door, her first greeting of the day being a frustrated, sharply issued order, without even a smile to soften her words.

Calli nodded once, unwilling to get into a familiar argument. Both women knew she wouldn't eat before leaving. Her stomach wouldn't wake up until half way through history in the third period, just in time for lunch. The doctor said she had to put weight on, but it was difficult when hunger evaded her for most of the day. The gluten free food which cost her parents an absolute fortune had a peculiar texture to it and resembled cardboard. The cereal was like something left at the bottom of a hay bale when you lifted it off the ground and her taste buds were only fooled during the first few bites.

Marcia grunted in frustration and whirled around on her heels, her full figure disappearing down the hallway. Calli relaxed and exhaled slowly. Marcia frightened her. The anti-depressants she had recently been shoving down her throat mellowed her a little more. She was less given to the loud and never ending lectures, mostly directed at Calli for some minor misdemeanour. It was good when Danny lived at home. He pulled faces behind her back and made Calli laugh, often getting her into even more trouble, but the sound of his whispers and that smirk which never failed to set her off giggling seemed like a distant memory now.

Calli bit her strawberry coloured lip to stifle the emotional pain. Danny died two years ago, his lithe, cyclist's body crushed by a passing truck which turned across him on his way home from school. Everything for a while after that was a dull blur in Calli's mind; his mangled bicycle and his creased, blood stained uniform, neatly folded by a medic's careful hands and dropped off by the police. His loss left a raw, open wound in Calli's soul; a cavernous insatiable pit of nothingness, which threatened constantly to suck her in and hold her there interminably. She hadn't dealt with it, because she had no idea where to start.

"Mum's angry," Jase announced, puffing back into the bedroom and shutting the door carelessly behind him. He hopped from foot to foot looking nervous and Calli instinctively reached out for his soft body and pulled it into hers. "Next door's doggie did another poop in our front garden. Dad's just trodden in it putting the bins out."

Calli rolled her eyes. Marcia detested the family next door with a passion, turning all of her unresolved grief in their direction without reservation. Their house towered above Calli's, and it was as though the shadow cast by their structure, reminded Marcia of the spectre of doom over her whole existence. She found fault in everything they did, which was awkward, as Calli shared most of her classes with the oldest son of the family. If their dog had defecated on the lawn, which she doubted as she hadn't seen or heard it for over six months, Marcia would never let it rest.

"Can you walk me, Calli Walli?" Jase begged as his sister did up the last buckle and sat up again, a look of reluctance in her face.

"It makes me late, Jase," she replied, her head already shaking out a determined no and tears formed in his eyes.

"Pleeeeeeease?" he whimpered, "Mum's being scary. I want you to take me. I'll walk as fast as fast can be, I promise and I won't do messing abouts on the way. I won't."

"No, Jase," Calli said firmly. "You haven't eaten breakfast yet or cleaned your teeth and we would have to leave right now."

Jase's eyes bulged excitedly in his head and he nodded frantically like a maniacal head-banger from the 1980's. "Had toast," he beamed victoriously and Calli saw the jam stain on his clean shirt."

"Teeth!" Her face was stern as she pointed towards the bathroom.

As Jase pelted noisily down the hallway, Calli noticed the flash of metal on her desk as the rays of the sun, already streaming in through her bedroom window, licked gently at the razor blade. Her father had put the bins out for collection by the sound of it and she didn't want the blade lounging in one of the house bins for a week because of Jase. She considered putting it in her pocket and binning it at school, but if she were discovered in possession of it, wrong conclusions would be drawn. It wasn't worth the hassle. Callister Rhodes already had something of a 'reputation.'

Pulling out her desk drawer, Calli found the battered little tin where she kept her treasures and dropped it in with a gentle plink. Jase could never get the lid off with his tiny finger joints straining and his little thumbs slipping on the surface. It would be safe there.

Grab A Trail of Lies here.

About the Author

K T Bowes is a bestselling teen and women's author. Her novel, *A Trail of Lies*, was the winner of the genre award for Author's Cave in 2014.

Phoenix Du Rose was considered for the prestigious Ngaio Marsh awards for 2021 and *Her Quiet Legacy* in 2022.

K T Bowes is an Englishwoman in exile in New Zealand, swapping rugged cosmopolitan for mountain ranges and terrifying rivers. She loves Māori culture and has learned to weave flax using traditional methods. Her other passion is Rongoa Māori, which involves creating medicines from native plants. She is a student of Te Reo Māori.

You can find her hanging out on social media in the following places.

Check in and say hello. Maybe suggest she gets back to writing and stops watching cat videos.

FACEBOOK

https://www.facebook.com/NZauthorKTBowes/

INSTAGRAM

https://www.instagram.com/k_t_bowes

Also by this Author

The Hana Du Rose Mysteries Series:
Logan Du Rose
About Hana
Hana Du Rose
Du Rose Legacy
The New Du Rose Matriarch
One Heartbeat
The Du Rose Prophecy
Du Rose Sons
Du Rose Family Ties
Du Rose Vendetta
Du Rose Blaze
The Hana Du Rose Mysteries; Generation Z
Phoenix Du Rose

Wiremu Du Rose

The Calculated Risk Series:

The Actuary

The Actuary's Wife

The Actuary in Trouble

The Heart of The Actuary

Troubled series for teens:

Free from the Tracks

Sophia's Dilemma

A Trail of Lies

Gone Phishing

Escaping the Back Country NZ Series:

Pirongia's Secret

Deleilah

Standalone novels:

Artifact

Demons on Her Shoulder

All Saints

Her Quiet Legacy

Humorous Cozy Mystery Series from New Zealand

Dead Straight

Bad Hair Day

Side Parting

www.ingramcontent.com/pod-product-compliance
Lightning Source LLC
LaVergne TN
LVHW030242250326
834688LV00047B/1762